JESSICA BECK
THE DONUT MYSTERIES, BOOK 57
JELLY-FILLED JUSTICE

Donut Mystery 57 JELLY-FILLED JUSTICE
Copyright © 2022 by Jessica Beck

The First Time Ever Published!
The 57th Donut Mystery!
JELLY-FILLED JUSTICE

Jessica Beck is the *New York Times* Bestselling Author of the Donut Mysteries, the Cast Iron Cooking Mysteries, the Classic Diner Mysteries, the Ghost Cat Cozy Mysteries, and more.

WHEN ARNIE LANCASTER gets out of prison on a technicality after being convicted of killing local Susie Mae Long, he comes to retired police chief Phillip Martin and donutmaker Suzanne Hart to figure out who really killed the woman sixteen years earlier. Is Arnie trying to whitewash his past, or did someone else really kill the woman and pin it on him?

To P and E,
Forever and Always.
And to all of you, Dear Readers,
Who've stuck with me through thick and thin.
I can't tell you how much I appreciate each and every one of you!

Chapter 1

"PHILLIP, ARNIE LANCASTER is out of prison, and he's back in town! He just bought a dozen donuts from me," I told my stepfather—retired chief of police of April Springs Phillip Martin—when he answered the front door of the cottage he shared with my mother. I'd left Emma in charge of Donut Hearts so I could rush over and tell him in person.

"I heard he was back in town twenty minutes ago. Chief Grant called me," Phillip said. "When I found out that they'd overturned his conviction last week on a technicality from the trial, I had a hunch he might come back to April Springs. So what?"

"So, he threatened to kill you back when he was convicted of murder! I don't know why he focused on you. You just arrested him. Judge Hackett was the one who put him away," I reminded him.

"I was an easy scapegoat, at least in Arnie's mind. We were fishing buddies, for land's sake! It was tough enough to arrest him, but I had no choice. The evidence pointed right at him. Suzanne, when I was chief of police in April Springs, I was threatened countless times."

"You seem awfully calm about this," I said, feeling a bit exasperated with the situation. "Would *you* come back to April Springs after all that happened if it were *you*? Aren't you even a *little* worried?"

My stepfather shrugged as he lifted his shirt to reveal the holstered gun on his hip. "I'm being cautious, but I'm not going to let it stop me from living my life."

"How about Momma?" I asked him. "Aren't you at least a little concerned about her?"

"Of course I am," he snapped at me, something that was rare these days, though when he'd been the police chief, he'd certainly had enough hard words with me. "But what can I do?"

"Send her away somewhere until we see how this plays out," I suggested.

He laughed, but there was no humor in it. "Really? Can you see your mother being sent *anywhere* she didn't want to be?"

"That's a fair point, but she needs to at least know what's going on," I told him.

"Trust me, she knows. Why do you think I'm wearing this?" Phillip asked as he gestured to the sidearm. "She promised me that she and Geneva would be careful."

Geneva Swift was becoming a friend of mine, slowly but surely. She'd taken the job as Momma's assistant after I'd turned down the position, and there had been some friction between us at first, but we were finally starting to warm up to each other. After all, we both had to deal with my mother's quirks and idiosyncrasies, which helped bring us closer together.

"Is that enough though?"

"It's all I can do, short of hiring Jake to be her bodyguard."

My husband—an ex–state police inspector and former chief of police in April Springs itself—had done a great many things in his career, but I doubted that babysitting was anything he cared to do too much of anymore. He'd tried helping out a few friends in the past working as a bodyguard, but it hadn't turned out very well. "Ordinarily, he wouldn't go for it, but if he knew that it was for Momma, I'm willing to bet that he'd be on board." My husband loved my mother dearly. I didn't *think* the pies and desserts she peppered him with were the only reasons, but they surely didn't hurt.

"I already ran the idea past your mother that it would be prudent to have Jake watching out for her."

"Do I even need to ask what her reaction was?" I asked him.

"I'm guessing you don't," Phillip said as his phone rang. "Hang on. It's your mother," he said, and then he stepped away to take it.

While he was chatting with her, I glanced at my stepfather's worktable, where he had several old newspaper clippings laid out, as well as half a dozen legal pads covered with all kinds of notes, questions, and ideas circled on them. My stepfather had retired from the police force and had quickly grown bored with an idle life. Most men took up woodworking or gardening later in life, but not Phillip. He'd developed a knack for investigating old and cold cases that most folks around April Springs had long forgotten. Jake, Momma, and I had even joined him on one of those old investigations, hunting for long-lost treasure that had disappeared.

"Well, that was fortuitous," Phillip said when he got off the phone and rejoined me.

"What happened? Has Arnie been arrested again already?" I asked, taking a stab in the dark.

"No, of course not. Dot and Geneva are leaving town for a few days after all."

I couldn't believe my mother would run away from trouble for one second, especially if her husband's safety were involved, despite what I'd just tried to convince Phillip to attempt.

"That doesn't sound like Momma," I said. "How did you manage to pull that off?"

"There's been a real estate investment opportunity in Virginia she's been working on for months, and she and Geneva are suddenly on a tight deadline to scope it out. They're heading out of town in a few hours."

"I'm honestly surprised she's leaving, what with Arnie showing up again and all, but I think it's for the best," I told him.

"She doesn't want to go, but I convinced her that if she stayed here, I'd be so worried about her that I might let my guard down and not be able to fully protect myself," he admitted.

"Is that true?"

"Does it matter? All that counts is that she's going," he answered.

"That doesn't answer my question," I pushed him.

Phillip clouded up. "Of course it's true, Suzanne! I'd *die* before I'd let your mother get hurt."

"I know that," I said as I touched his shoulder lightly. "Still, Jake should be involved in this."

"Your mother called him before she called me," he admitted with a grin. "He'll be over here any second."

At that moment, I heard a truck pull up into the driveway. I knew Phillip was perfectly capable of handling himself, but it made me feel a great deal better knowing that Jake would be around, too.

"Jake, as much as I like seeing you, you didn't have to rush over here," Phillip said when he answered the door before I could say a word.

"I was on my way out of town, but I'm going to cancel my trip," my husband said. "My sister will understand."

I was glad he'd offered to help, because I'd been about to ask him to do it myself. I loved his sister and her kids, but the feeling wasn't all that mutual. Sarah seemed much happier when I stayed in April Springs and Jake visited her alone in Raleigh. She always threatened to come visit us, but it had never materialized, though we were less than four hours away.

"I have had just about enough of being babied," Phillip said, his face drawn into a frown. "I can barely tolerate it from my wife, but not you two. Jake, I'm perfectly safe."

"I don't know about that," Jake said before he glanced in my direction. "Suzanne? What do you think? You saw this Arnie Lancaster character. How did he seem to you at the donut shop?"

"Honestly, he seemed fine. That was what had me so worried," I told the two former police chiefs.

"How do you mean?" Jake asked.

"The man just got out of prison, he comes back to April Springs, and the first thing he does is buy a dozen donuts? I don't think so. It just doesn't make sense. My treats are good, but they aren't 'get out of prison and splurge' good."

"What makes you think coming to see you was the *first* thing he did?" Phillip asked me.

I looked at him for a second before I smiled. "You're right. I have no idea what he's done since he's gotten back into town, but it had to be this morning. Otherwise, at least one of my customers would have told me about it."

"Are you that confident in your personal grapevine?" Jake asked me.

"Yeah, I'm pretty sure somebody would have made it a point to tell me if they'd seen Arnie hanging around."

"Fine. He came back to town. Again, so what? The court says he's a free man," Phillip said. "There's really nothing we can do about it."

"I can hang around town for a while and watch your back," Jake said solemnly. "At least for a few days until we see which way the wind is blowing."

"I appreciate that, and when and if I ever need to be protected in the future, you're on my speed dial." He paused a moment and then asked, "Jake, how many folks did you put away while you were on the job?"

My husband rubbed his cheek for a moment in thought, and then he said, "I don't have a hard number."

"But it has to be in the dozens. Right?"

"Oh, yes," Jake replied. I knew he wasn't bragging. He'd been responsible for making North Carolina a safer place for years, but I also knew that it had come at a price.

"And how many of them have come after you when they got out?" Phillip pushed.

"Two," Jake admitted.

I knew about one of them, but he hadn't told me about the other. "Really? Jake Bishop, have you been holding out on me all this time?"

"Suzanne, it's in the past, and that's where I'd like to keep it," Jake said dismissively. "Besides, it was way before I met you. I never saw any reason to bring it up."

"What happened, Jake? Don't you think I have a right to know?" I pushed him.

"This isn't about me. It's about Phillip," my husband answered, clearly not interested in talking about it.

Well, that was just too bad. "Phillip can wait," I said, and then I shot a look of apology toward my stepfather.

"I agree wholeheartedly," Phillip said. "What happened, Jake?"

He took a deep breath, and then he let it out slowly before he began to tell the story. "I put a woman away for grand larceny. By the time she got out, she'd built me up in her head as the villain of her life story. The moment she got out, she ambushed me at my apartment complex. The woman took a shot at me and missed, and then she wouldn't drop the weapon, even after I practically begged her to. Evidently, prison made her meaner and crazier than she'd been when she'd gone in."

"What happened?" I asked softly.

"She was getting ready to fire again, screaming at me that I was a dead man. I had no choice. I shot her," Jake said succinctly.

"Was it a kill shot?" Phillip asked him.

Jake nodded. "Like I said, I had no choice. It was pretty clear that she was determined to kill me, so I had to act. It was her or me."

"It sounds like you did the only thing you could do," I told him, wishing that I'd just left it alone. Jake had a reason for not wanting to re-live that particular nightmare, and I'd forced his hand. Honestly, some-times I think I'm a mature, reasonable adult, and then there are other times when I feel like a complete and total idiot. "I'm so sorry," I said lamely.

"Like I said, it's in the past, Suzanne," he said, but I could still see the pain in his eyes from the memory.

I promised myself that, in the future, if Jake didn't want to talk about something from his life before me, I would drop it. At least I'd try to.

Sometimes even knowing the right thing to do isn't the same thing as doing it.

"That's my point, Phillip," Jake continued. "You just never know."

"I'm sorry you went through that, and if it happens to me I'll deal with it, but I'm not hiding behind the two of you. Do you understand?"

I was about to protest when the doorbell rang.

Jake started toward the door, but Phillip put a hand on his shoulder. "It's my house. I'll answer my own door, thank you very much."

My stepfather did at least glance through the peephole before he opened the door.

Whatever he saw there clearly caught him off guard.

"It's Arnie Lancaster," Phillip said, obviously unsettled by the man's presence on his doorstep after all those years.

Chapter 2

"LET ME HANDLE THIS," Jake said as he tried to step past Phillip.

"I said I've got it," my stepfather said firmly as he opened the door. "Arnie. Long time no see."

"Hey, Phil. Got a second?" he asked as he looked past Phillip directly at Jake and then me. Phil? I'd never heard him called that in my life, but like he'd said, the two men had a long history. Arnie was a handsome man, with a full head of hair and a ready smile. There was something about him that made him older than his years though, as though he'd experienced more than his share of misery in his life, which I supposed was accurate.

"Sure. Is this a front-porch thing or a living-room thing?" Phillip asked him.

"Your call. I brought you some donuts, you know, you being a cop and all," he said with a slight grin as he offered them to my stepfather.

"Retired cop. Thanks," Phillip said, taking them from him but not opening the box. "I may have one later."

"You lost weight, my friend," Arnie said. If I hadn't known the history between the two men, it would have seemed like a normal conversation, but given what had happened in the past, I was befuddled by the exchange. "In case you hadn't noticed, I have, too," Arnie said, "but for a different reason. I was sorry to hear about Evelyn."

"Which part, the divorce or what happened later? It doesn't matter. Thanks. I'm married to Dot Hart these days."

"Thus the weight loss, I'm guessing. It seems to suit you." Arnie took a deep breath, and then he added, "I came by to say that I'm sorry about threatening you in court. I wasn't in my right mind. You were just doing your job. You thought I was guilty, and you did what you had to do."

"Well, that's pretty forgiving of you," Phillip said, clearly a bit skeptical about the man's change of heart.

"Let's just say that I had some time to think about things while I was inside," Arnie said. "That brings me to the second reason I'm here. I need your help."

"What can I do for you?" Phillip asked. "I'm not the police chief anymore. If it's money you're looking for, I don't have much."

Arnie cut him off. "I'm set, thanks. My pop passed away while I was inside and left me enough to keep me set for life, as long as I'm careful with it."

"Then what can I do to help?"

"I need you to find out who really killed Susie Mae Long," he said.

"Are you serious?" Phillip asked him. "Arnie, I know you got out on a technicality, but I stand by the evidence. You were seen arguing with Susie Mae in public three hours before the murder. Not only that, but she owed you money when you broke up, and we all know about that temper of yours. Arnie, I'm not sure I can do anything for you."

"That's just it though. It was no secret that we were having problems, and that fight *was* pretty public. Someone took advantage of that fact and killed Susie so they could frame me for it. They did a pretty fine job of it, too. If you help me solve the case, then folks around here won't hold it against me for the rest of my life," Arnie said, almost pleading.

"You could go somewhere else and start fresh," I suggested. I'd known Arnie briefly, but as a child might know an adult.

"I know you sold me those donuts, but I'm not quite sure what you're doing here," Arnie said.

"This is Dot's daughter, Suzanne," Phillip said, and then he turned to Jake. "And this is her husband, State Police Inspector Jake Bishop."

"Retired state police inspector," Jake corrected him.

Arnie offered his hand, but Jake just stood there and stared at him. It was clear whose side he was on, as if there was any doubt about it.

"See?" Arnie asked, not taking offense at the refusal as he put his hand away. "He doesn't even know me, and he won't shake my hand. I can't live like this."

"Suzanne asked you a fair question," Jake followed up. "Why come back to April Springs when there's so much history here?"

"That's just it: it's my history. This is where my folks are buried, where I grew up, and where I had a life a long time ago. I'm not letting someone else take that from me, too."

"What else did they take from you?" I asked.

"My good name and sixteen years of my life," Arnie said.

Oddly enough, I believed him. In the past, I'd been wrong a few times about people, but my gut was usually pretty good when it came to sizing up guilt and innocence. After all, if he was telling us the truth, why else would he want the past murder investigated if there was a chance it just would prove that he actually had done it and had gotten away on a technicality?

"I don't know," Phillip said, frowning. "Let me think about it and talk to a few folks first, okay?"

"Sure, but don't take too long. I need you, Phil, and if I'm telling the truth, don't you think you at least owe me that much to help me clear my name?" When there was no response, he added, "I'm at Pop's old place. I hope you help me, Phil. I honestly do."

As he was leaving on foot, Momma and Geneva pulled up in her car. My mother rushed in before we had a chance to discuss Arnie's request or what Phillip should do about it.

"Was that Arnie Lancaster?" she asked. "What was he doing here?"

"Believe it or not, he came by to apologize," Phillip said.

"He asked Phillip for help clearing his name," I added.

"He has lost his mind completely," Momma said as Geneva joined us after parking the car. "You're not going to do it, are you?" she asked him curtly.

"I'm not sure," he said.

"You can't be serious. Phillip Martin, I forbid it. Do you understand me? I forbid it!" My mother was using a tone of voice on him that I'd heard a lot during my teenage years. It hadn't sat well with me, and it was clearly not about to fly with my stepfather, either.

"Dot, I need to have a word with you. In private."

"Anything you have to say to me can be said in front of everyone here," Momma said, digging her heels in. She evidently didn't think Phillip had the stones to confront her in front of an audience.

"If you'll excuse me, I've got some last-second travel arrangements to see to," Geneva said as she started for the door.

"Stay," Momma and Phillip said simultaneously. I'd been about to try to get out of witnessing the argument myself, but after seeing the way they'd shut Geneva down, I knew that I didn't stand a chance. I was going to be a witness to the confrontation, whether I wanted to be or not.

"Dot, I love you more than life itself, and when you agreed to marry me, it was the happiest day of my life, bar none. But..."

"There's no need to qualify that with a but," Momma said.

"You're wrong, about that and about giving me ultimatums in general. I'm not a lapdog, woman! An old friend has come to me for help, and I'm going to do it!"

"You're just agreeing to help him because I told you not to," Momma said a bit indignantly.

"That may be part of it," Phillip said in a calmer manner, "but it's certainly not the entire reason. What if he's telling the truth? I played a key role in getting him locked up! If I made a mistake all those years ago and played a part in a miscarriage of justice, I have to fix it if I can."

"Jake, would you please talk some sense into him?" Momma asked my husband.

"I'm sorry, Dot, but I have to agree with Phillip. If I were in his shoes, I would do the exact same thing."

That clearly wasn't what Momma had been hoping to hear. "Suzanne? Can *you* try to talk sense into these men?"

"Momma, you need to drop it. You're not going to win this argument," I told her gently. "We both married lawmen, and they live by a different code than we do. That's something that's been pointed out to me on more than one occasion, and I'm finally starting to understand it."

My mother clearly couldn't believe it when her only child wouldn't back her up, either. "I see I'm wasting my time and my breath here, then. Geneva, make those arrangements. We're leaving in one hour." It was as cold and abrupt as I'd heard her in many years, and I hated to see it directed at her husband.

If Phillip was hurt by it, he hid it well. "I'll help you pack," he said.

"Don't bother," Momma answered as she headed for their bedroom.

Phillip chose to ignore another of her commands and followed her anyway.

Once they were out of the room, Geneva said, "I've got to go pack myself. If anyone asks, tell them that I'll be back shortly."

"Sorry you had to witness that," I told her.

"Witness what? I didn't see a thing," Geneva answered with a slight grin. "That was one of the first things I learned working for your mother. I'll be back soon."

And then she was gone as well.

"So, what do we do now?" Jake asked. "Do we sit around and wait for them to come out, or do we go home?"

"You can do what you want, but I'm going to see if there's any pie," I told him as I headed for the kitchen.

"You're just going to invite yourself to dessert before you've even had lunch?" Jake asked me, smiling slightly.

"Hey, I figure anything I find in this house is fair game," I said as I dug into the fridge. "Oh, wow, score!" I said as I brought a lidded glass container out of the fridge. "It's bread pudding."

"I *love* bread pudding," Jake said, looking longingly at the dessert.

"Grab two plates and some forks, then. I'll get a big spoon out. Now, if she's got vanilla ice cream, I'll be set."

"*We'll* be set, you mean," Jake said with a full-blown grin now.

"Hey, I was saving that for later," Phillip protested a few minutes later when he and Momma joined us in the kitchen.

"I made a fresh batch this morning, and I even dropped some off at your house, Suzanne," Momma said. She'd clearly been crying, but she was smiling now, and she and Phillip seemed to be getting along just fine. If they wanted to pretend that nothing had happened, that was fine with me. "There's enough for everyone, though it is awfully early for such a rich dessert."

"Then you don't have to have any," Phillip said as he kissed her cheek.

"Let's not get carried away," Momma said with a grin.

"Two more plates it is, then," Phillip answered with a laugh. "I see you found the ice cream, Suzanne."

"Was there ever any doubt in your mind?" I asked as I took a bite. "Bread pudding is great cold, but I love heating it up enough to make the ice cream melt a little."

"I'll eat it however I can get it," Jake answered.

As Momma took a bite from the plate Phillip had provided her, she said, "We've come to a decision. Phillip is going to help Arnie."

"Okay," Jake said. "We can do that."

"*You*, sir, are going to Raleigh as planned," Momma told him. "I want *Suzanne* to help him solve this case."

Jake was clearly surprised by that edict. "Dot, need I remind you that I'm a trained investigator? Suzanne is amazing, but I've worked my entire life doing this kind of thing."

"I hate to disagree with you, but in fact, you've done just the opposite. You've been on the adversarial side of things. As a police officer, you look for new evidence, but to convict your suspect, not exonerate him."

"What if there *is* no evidence after all this time?" Jake asked her.

"That's where Suzanne comes in. People tell her things they would *never* tell a police officer, and like it or not, most people can tell within minutes that the two of you were once in uniform. Suzanne can balance that out with her more approachable manner."

"Do I get a say in this, or am I being drafted without my consent?" I asked. "I'm not refusing to help. I'm just curious."

Momma looked surprised by my question. "Suzanne Hart, when have you *ever* refused to work on a murder case in your life?"

"That's not the point. A girl likes to be asked; that's all."

Phillip released his fork long enough to grasp my free hand with both of his. "Suzanne Hart, will you help me investigate this cold case? Please?"

"Oh, stop it," I said, giggling at his mock earnestness. "Of course I'll help you." I took my hand back from him and turned to Jake. "You don't mind, do you?"

"No, actually, it makes perfect sense. Your mother is right," Jake said.

"You should take more after your husband, young lady," Momma told me.

"I often think you're right, Momma." She was about to say something when I finished my sentiment. "Just not all the time, no matter what you believe."

"I'll take what I can get," Momma said as she started gathering dirty dishes. "Now, if you'll excuse me, I've got a trip to prepare for. I have just a few more things to pack, and then I'll be ready to go."

"Hang on a second," I said. "I'll help you."

I tagged along as she walked back to her bedroom. As Momma finished packing, she said, "Suzanne, I really don't need any supervision."

"That's up for debate, but what I really want is to know how Phillip convinced you that he was right and you were wrong."

"How is that any possible concern of yours?" Momma asked me.

"Call it research for a later date," I told her with a grin. "I could use the tip."

"You never change, do you?" Momma asked, returning my smile with one of her own.

"Oh, that's debatable, but seriously, what did Phillip say to convince you?"

"He told me that his biggest nightmares have always been about the people who might have been innocent that he helped put in jail," my mother told me. "I knew that he occasionally had bad dreams about something, but I didn't realize that was what they concerned."

"I get that, but Arnie could just be using this as an excuse to get close to Phillip so he can kill him," I told her somberly.

"That's why I want you to be my eyes and ears," Momma said. "Protect my husband, Suzanne. Please."

"Wouldn't Jake be more qualified to do that than I am?" I asked her, wary about the responsibility I'd apparently just assumed.

"Perhaps, but my other reason for wanting you on the case stands. You have a way with people. You can get them to talk about things that the police never could. Just keep an eye on Arnie while you're doing it."

"I'll do my best," I told her.

"I know you will," she said as she hugged me. I was never more aware of my mother's diminutive stature than I was when we shared an embrace. It was ironic that this powerhouse of a woman had been given such a slight body, but there was nothing slight about her presence. "I'm counting on you, young lady."

"I won't let you down," I said.

"Excellent. Now, let me finish this. Unless I'm mistaken, that's Geneva pulling up now."

"Good luck on your business trip," I told her.

"I believe the correct phrase is 'break a leg,'" she told me.

"Break whatever you want to," I said. "Try not to worry too much while you're gone."

"I've been a worrier since the day you were born," Momma admitted. "Motherhood has a way of doing that to you."

"You worry about *me*? Really? I'm just a simple donutmaker. What possible kind of trouble can *I* get into?" I asked her mischievously.

"Don't get me started, my darling daughter. We simply don't have the time."

Chapter 3

WHEN WE WALKED BACK into the living room, our husbands were deep in discussion about something. "What's up, you two?" I asked.

"We've been trying to come up with some ideas about how to tackle the situation," Jake told me.

"Have you had any luck?" Momma asked.

"Unfortunately, it looks as though we're going to have to just play it by ear," Phillip answered.

"Oh, goody. That's what I do best," I said.

"What have I gotten myself into?" Phillip asked with mock remorse, but it was clear he was happy to be working with me on a case again.

"Actually, *I* got you into it," Momma told him just before kissing him soundly. "Now take care of yourself, do you hear me? If anything happens to either one of you, I don't know what I would do."

"Hey, what about me?" Jake asked her with a grin.

"You should be just fine, but if it makes you feel any better, I care deeply about all three of you."

Geneva came in as Momma was kissing Jake's cheek, and she actually looked a bit embarrassed by the display of affection. I couldn't help myself, so I said, "I can't turn my back on these two before they start carrying on so brazenly."

"Suzanne Hart, you know perfectly well that I..." After a split second, Momma added, "Find your humor lacking at times. Hello, Geneva. Are we set?"

"Ready to go, Dot," she said.

"Then let's not tarry," Momma told her. She hugged Jake, gave me a hug and a kiss, and then embraced her husband and kissed him mightily once more before leaving.

I was afraid Geneva's head might explode. It was clear she wasn't all that comfortable with public displays of affection of any kind.

"Take care, you," Momma said softly to her husband.

"You do the same," Phillip answered in the same timbre.

"I'm not the one digging into a murder," she told him.

"No, but you're going to be swimming with sharks just the same."

"Ah, but you forget. I'm the biggest shark of them all," Momma said with a grin.

"You're not telling me anything I don't already know. Knock 'em dead," he said, and then he slapped her bottom.

Momma laughed, much to Geneva's surprise, and honestly, a bit of mine too. It just went to show how nervous my mother was about leaving her husband in what she considered a dangerous situation.

"Don't sweat it," he said. "I've got this, Dot."

"*We've* got it," I corrected him.

"Right. *We*," Phillip added with a nod.

"Dot, I'll walk you out," Jake said. "I suppose I'd better get on the road myself."

"I'll go with you," I told him, and then I turned to my stepfather. "I'll be right back."

"Okay, but don't take too long. We've got a murder to solve. Or not."

"Hey, you said good-bye to your spouse. Now it's my turn," I told him.

"Point taken," Phillip answered.

After seeing Momma and Geneva off, I hugged my husband and gave him a kiss that would surely have knocked Geneva unconscious if she'd seen it.

"Wow, I should leave more often," Jake said with a grin as he pulled away.

"Thanks for understanding about all of this," I told him.

"Hey, I get it. The best man for this job is actually a woman."

"Don't sound so surprised. It's been my experience that's *usually* the case," I told him with a grin.

"I couldn't agree more," Jake answered. "I'll call you when I get to Sarah's place."

"You'd better. Safe travels."

"I'll be fine. Watch your back, and Phillip's, too," Jake said as he got into his truck.

"You bet," I said.

I stood there waving until he vanished out of sight, and then I headed back inside.

Or at least I started to.

Phillip came out the front door with a satchel under his arm before I had a chance to go back inside.

"Were you spying on me?" I asked him with a grin.

"I never got to do it when you were a teenager. It's kind of a stepfather's rite of passage, isn't it?"

"It probably is," I agreed. "So, are you ready to go talk to Arnie?"

"I am if you are," he said as he headed for his truck.

"Why don't I drive?" I asked as I got into my Jeep without waiting for his approval. He really had no choice but to follow suit, and once we were both buckled up, I said, "By the way, we'll probably pick up something to eat soon if that's your lunch."

"It's the old case file on Susie Mae Long," he said. "I made a copy before I retired."

"Did you do that with *all* of your cases?" I asked him. He'd been our chief of police for a long time, so I couldn't imagine how much storage that would take.

"No, just the ones that bothered me a bit at the time," he admitted.

"So then you weren't completely convinced that Arnie killed Susie Mae?"

"Like I said, I had enough to arrest him, and that was all I needed," Phillip answered.

"That didn't address the question," I pointed out.

He just shrugged. "It's not hard to spend time second-guessing yourself in that job. Let's go talk to Arnie."

As I headed over there, I realized that those files did more to convince me that Arnie might be innocent than anything the man himself had said. If Phillip hadn't been one hundred percent certain that he'd arrested the right man, then there was enough uncertainty to at least give Arnie the benefit of the doubt.

Arnie Lancaster was outside, sanding the front porch steps of his father's house when we drove up.

"You came," he said with a grin. It faded a bit when he spotted me tagging along. "Hello, Suzanne," he added a bit warily.

"Hi," I said.

"Arnie, there's something you should know from the start. We're a package deal, so if you have a problem with Suzanne helping, then this is where we part ways. She might be a donutmaker by trade, and a darned fine one at that, but she also happens to be the best amateur sleuth in these parts that I've ever seen."

"If you keep that up, you're going to make me blush," I told my stepfather. I was grateful for the praise and the fact that he'd just stood up for me. We'd come a long way indeed since he'd been the chief of police for April Springs.

"I'm happy you can help, Suzanne," Arnie said. "As soon as I left you all, I did a little digging, and I found out that you are the real deal. I welcome anything you can do to help."

"Well, I don't sand porch steps, if that's what you're asking," I said, trying to break the tension of the situation. I wasn't sure if he was innocent or not, but until we started digging into the cold case, I would *never* know. My gut, for what it was worth, trusted the man, at least so far. I'd have to watch that. First, I needed a reason to trust him, and I didn't have that, at least not yet.

"No, I'm happy to do the home renovations myself. Pop let this place go, but I mean to bring it back to all of its former glory."

I studied the modest house and wondered if it had ever been a showplace. I didn't say it, but clearly, Arnie read my mind. "Okay, it never was the top of the line, but I grew up here, and I love this old house. Trust me, she can look a lot better than she does now."

"Good for you," I said. "Should we do this out here, inside, or maybe go by my donut shop? Emma has no doubt finished cleaning up by now."

"I could use a bite," Arnie admitted. "Any chance there are any donuts left over?"

"I don't know, but I can ask," I said as I pulled out my phone and called Emma.

"I just left the bank," Emma said when she knew that it was me. "I didn't know what to do with the extras, so I'm taking most of them to class with me if that's okay."

"That's fine," I said. "Are you going to see Jason?" I added coyly. Emma had broken up with her fiancé a few months earlier, and one of her classmates had been doing his best to woo her ever since. I wasn't sure how much encouragement she'd given him, but he was making himself available to her, just in case. I liked the young man, but I had promised myself to stay out of it. At least a little longer, anyway.

"Yes, he sits next to me every class," she said.

"And is that a good thing or a bad thing?" I asked, not able to help myself.

"I don't think it's going to rain, but you can never be sure this time of year," she answered brightly.

"In other words, mind my own business," I said with a laugh. "Are you still coming in tomorrow?"

"Unless you want to change the schedule and give me an extra day off," Emma said with a laugh.

"No, we're good. I'll see you then," I told her. "Enjoy class. By the way, Jason likes glazed donuts, in case you were wondering."

"I know. He told me last week that they should bottle the way I smell after a shift at the donut shop as perfume. He said there wasn't a man alive who could resist it. I told him that I'd found more than my fair share who could over the years, none of them all that great, and he told me that I was just hanging around with the wrong guys. I couldn't dispute that, could I?"

I was about to say something when Phillip caught my eye. He and Arnie were clearly getting impatient, so I wrapped things up. "Talk to you soon. Thanks again for covering for me this morning."

"Hey, it's what I do," she said with a laugh. I knew that her breakup with Barton Gleason, the egotistical chef, had been rough on her, but it felt to me as though she was coming out on the other side of it. Maybe Jason might have a shot after all.

"Sorry, it sounds as though most of the leftover donuts are gone," I told them as I dialed another number. "But I have another idea if you two trust me."

"Always," Phillip answered promptly.

"If he's good with it, then so am I," Arnie answered.

Trish picked up. "Boxcar Grill."

"Hey. Any chance I can get three specials, to go, in about five minutes?" I asked her.

"Wow, how hungry *are* you?" she asked with a laugh. "Or is it for just Grace and you?"

"Grace is at a conference in Las Vegas," I told her.

"So you're going to eat all *three* of them?" Trish teased me. "Don't try to tell me that one or two are for Jake. He stopped by earlier and got a bite before he left town."

"Hey, I have *other* friends in my life," I protested.

"Besides me, you mean? Wow, you really *are* popular. Three specials to go. They'll be ready when you get here."

"Thanks," I told her.

"Let's go over to Donut Hearts, where we can talk," I said. "But we need to make one stop along the way at the Boxcar. Are the specials good enough for lunch?"

"Perfect," both men said in near unison.

"Wow, we're already agreeing on something, at least," I said.

"I get it," Arnie said as soon as the three of us were in the Jeep.

"Get what?" I asked him.

"Why you got those orders to go," he said. "I don't blame you a bit, Suzanne. If it were me, I wouldn't want to be seen with me, either."

I didn't say anything until we got to the Boxcar. After I got out, I turned to the two men still sitting in the Jeep. "Come on. I'm not waiting all day."

"I thought you ordered our food to go?" Phillip asked.

"I did, until Arnie thought I was ashamed of being seen with him. Now it's a matter of principle with me."

"Suzanne, you don't know me from Adam. This is unnecessary."

"Maybe for you it is, but not for me," I told him. "Now, if you two care to join me, I'll be inside. Otherwise, you can get your own food." I turned and headed up the stairs, trusting that they would follow. If we were going to do this, we were going to do it right, and that meant that folks around April Springs might as well get used to seeing the three of us together. Sure, my reputation might take a hit being seen with the convicted murderer, but it had taken worse hits in the past, and I was certain it would again. Nobody, and I mean nobody, was going to have any reason to feel as though I were ashamed of being seen with them, and if folks didn't like it, that was just too bad.

Maybe Momma was right. She often accused me of looking for fights when there weren't any to be found, but I had a feeling she'd be proud of me for doing what I was doing at the moment, and that was really all that mattered to me.

Chapter 4

"HEY, SUZANNE," TRISH said with a smile. "I was wondering where you were. With Jake and Grace both out of town, it makes sense for you to eat here." Her smile vanished when Arnie Lancaster walked in, but when she saw Phillip behind him, her expression shifted to confusion. It was time to let the town know what was going on, and short of taking out an ad in Ray Blake's rag of a newspaper, announcing something in the Boxcar Grill was good enough for me.

"Phillip and I are working with Arnie to see if we can figure out what really happened to Susie Mae Long," I said. Usually, I liked to keep a low profile when I investigated, but this was an exception.

"We all *know* what happened," Parker Henson said as he threw his check and a twenty-dollar bill at Trish as he stormed out.

"Come back soon," Trish called out to him.

"I'm so sorry," I told Trish. "I hate that you're losing customers over us. We could stick with the to-go order and get out of your hair."

"Are you kidding?" Trish asked, brightening up. "Parker just tipped me thirty-five percent, and usually, I'm lucky to get whatever spare change he's got in his pocket. You know the drill. Find yourself a table, and I'll be right over, unless you still want these," she said as she gestured to the bag on the counter, waiting for us.

"Sorry about that," I said as Marvin Whitehurst came in a rush.

"I need three specials to go, as soon as you can make them," he said, nearly out of breath.

"Is that soon enough?" Trish asked as she handed him the bag.

"What? How long has this been sitting here?" Marvin asked with one eyebrow askew.

"It just came out. We had a last-second cancellation. Do you want it or not?"

"I'll take it," he said as he gave her the money.

"Problem solved," Trish said after Marvin was gone.

"I wish all my problems could be fixed that easily," I told her.

"Get in line, sister. We all do," Trish answered as she winked at me.

We took a table in back, hoping that we'd attract less attention there, but it was not to be. George Morris, our mayor and a former police officer, walked into the diner and came over to our table without even slowing down at Trish's station up front. He sat down in the empty fourth chair and stared at the released convict for a few seconds before he spoke. "Arnie," he said, ignoring us for the moment.

"George," Arnie said curtly.

"It's *Mayor Morris* to you," he answered just as snippily.

"*George*," I said, emphasizing his first name. "We're going to dig into this. I'm sorry if you don't like it, but it's something we have to do."

"Don't forget that I worked on the case *with* you, Phillip," George told his former boss, ignoring me again. "You and I both know that it was a clean arrest. We got the right guy the first time. If the courts decided to let him out, that has nothing to do with what we did."

"Then it won't hurt digging into the case again all these years later," my stepfather told him evenly.

"That's where you're wrong. It's going to bring up a lot of bad memories for a great many people, but I can't stop you, even though I think you're wasting your time," he said as he stood, but before he left, he leaned over Arnie and said softly, "I'll be watching you."

"Nice seeing you, Mayor Morris," Arnie said, keeping his expression devoid of any emotion.

"Yeah, right," George said, and then he left the diner without eating.

"That went well," I said sardonically.

"If you mean he didn't grab me by the throat and choke me, you're right," Arnie said.

"I take it there's some bad blood there," I said.

"He was sweet on Susie Mae," Arnie explained, "and he could never figure out why she chose me over him."

That certainly shed a little light on his open hostility toward the man. "Susie Mae had quite the fan club, not just our mayor," Phillip said. "Even you have to admit that you weren't an obvious match."

Arnie shrugged. "Hey, I knew she was out of my league, but if she didn't mind, why should I? I figured she was slumming it dating a day laborer when she could have done a lot better."

"Is that why she broke up with you?" I asked him.

Arnie just shrugged.

"Hey, I'm not asking out of morbid curiosity," I said, pushing him a little harder. "I'd like an answer. It's relevant to the case."

Arnie glanced at Phillip, who nodded. "I wouldn't mind hearing that myself."

"Fine. She dumped me. She said she was tired of always paying everywhere we went. It happened one time! I told her I would have money if she'd just pay me back the cash I'd loaned her, but she just laughed at me. She said I could kiss that money good-bye."

"That must have been tough for you to take," I said.

"It wasn't easy. Was I mad? Sure. Upset enough to kill her? No, not on your life. I know I had a temper back then, but it's mostly gone now. Prison has a way of beating it out of you. I was mainly upset with myself for giving her the money in the first place."

"How much are we talking about here?" I asked him as Trish approached with a tray laden with plates. She'd dropped off our drinks earlier.

"A thousand bucks," he said.

"Hey, I know inflation is hitting all of us, but your bill isn't going to be that much," Trish said. "Let me get you some refills on those drinks."

As Trish puttered around, I thought about a thousand dollars as a motive for murder. I knew that was the equivalent of quite a bit more money today, but it still wasn't enough to kill for, at least not in my book.

Once Trish was gone, I asked, "Why don't we eat and then continue this discussion at Donut Hearts?"

"Sounds good to me," Arnie said as he dug into the country-style steak, mashed potatoes, and fried okra. "Wow, this is incredible."

"It's good," I agreed as I took a bite myself.

"You don't understand what I've been eating. This is fit for a king."

"Then enjoy it, your highness," I said as I saw yet another denizen of April Springs approach our table.

This wasn't going to be good.

It was Gabby Williams, the town's biggest grump.

Gabby surprised me by smiling at Arnie and sitting across from him. "I just heard the good news. I'm glad you made it out."

"So am I," Arnie said. "How have you been, Gabby?"

"I've had better days," she admitted, "like today, seeing you again after all these years."

"I take it you two know each other?" I asked her.

"Arnie and I have been friends for twenty-five years," she said. "I knew he didn't kill Susie Mae even back then, but nobody would listen to me." As she said the last bit, she shifted her focus to Phillip.

"You had a gut feeling, Gabby," he explained. "Without any hard evidence to back it up, it didn't do me any good."

"Since when have my instincts *not* been spot on the money?" Gabby asked him.

I could think of at least three times in our shared past that she'd been dead wrong about things, but I decided to keep that to myself.

"Like I said, I needed evidence," Phillip answered.

"You're looking for some now though, aren't you?" Gabby asked with a penetrating look.

"Wow, word travels fast," I said. "I just told Trish not ten minutes ago."

"I didn't hear it from anybody, Suzanne. I'm a smart woman. I put two and two together. You and Phillip are here in public with Arnie. That means you believe that he's innocent and you're trying to clear his good name. I was friends with Susie Mae, and I want to see who really killed her caught and behind bars myself."

"You got half of that right," Phillip said. "We're digging into the murder again, but we're not convinced that Arnie didn't do it."

She started to protest when Arnie held up a hand. "Hold on. He's right, Gabby. I expect he and Suzanne will do their best to find the truth, something that can only help me, since I *know* that I didn't do it."

"I'm glad you're working on it too, Suzanne," Gabby told me.

"Momma kind of volunteered me," I told her.

"So you're doing this under duress?" she asked me pointedly.

"No, I'm happy to help, but I'm doing it for Phillip, not Arnie."

"Hey, either way, I win, so I'm not complaining," Arnie said with a smile.

"Unless we find more evidence that you actually did it," I told him, meeting his gaze with my own.

"He can't be tried again for it though," Gabby pointed out. "There's something called double jeopardy, right?"

"That's true enough, but I want to live here again in peace and quiet, so all I care about is what everyone else thinks," Arnie admitted.

"Well, there you might be in trouble," Gabby said with a frown. "Most folks are still convinced that you did it." That was Gabby, telling the truth, at least as she saw it, regardless of the consequences or even her own feelings.

"Well, maybe they'll change their minds when we find the real killer," Arnie answered.

"If, and it's a pretty big if, Arnie," Phillip said with a frown.

"Hey, at least you two are going to try, which was a whole lot more than I had when I woke up this morning."

"Well, I'll let you get to it, then," Gabby said as she stood. She plucked the check up from the table as she did. "This is on me."

"You don't have to do that, Gabby," Arnie said.

"I know. That's what makes it fun," she replied.

Once she was gone, I said, "Wow, you've got a fan in Gabby, and there aren't many folks in April Springs who can say that."

"We went out a few times," he admitted, shedding new light on my friend's earlier life.

"Do you mean you dated?" I asked, my incredulity there for the world to see.

"Hey, she's a handsome woman, and I'm a man. What's so crazy about that?"

"I'm guessing you dated her before you started going out with Susie Mae," I said. "Was it right before, by any chance?"

"Yeah, now that I think about it. How did you know that, and what does it matter?" Arnie asked me.

"Did *you* break up with *her*, or did *she* dump *you*?" I asked, ignoring his question.

"I'm the one who ended it. Why does it matter all these years later?"

"Because you just gave Gabby Williams a motive to want to kill Susie Mae Long," I told him. "If she thought that getting rid of her competition was the only way to get you back, it might have led to murder."

"Suzanne, you don't believe that for one second, do you?" Phillip asked me.

"I surely don't want to, but we need to look into it. While we're discussing suspects, George has to be on the list, too."

"The mayor?" Arnie asked, clearly surprised by the addition.

"I don't think he did it any more than Gabby did, but he was clearly jealous of your relationship with Susie Mae."

"That would make him want to kill *me*, not *her*, right?" Arnie asked, his remaining bit of food left untouched.

"What if he went to her and asked her to dump you before she did? Who knows, maybe he planted the seed in her mind. Once he found out she'd done it, he'd assumed she'd done it for him. If she rejected him after learning that, he might have been angry enough to kill her." Even as I said it, I didn't believe it, but we owed it to the dead woman to investigate every nook and cranny of the case, and if that meant putting the spotlight on some of our friends, then that was just how it had to be.

"I don't know," Arnie said. "Phillip, what do you think?"

"I think Suzanne is right. We need to dig into every possible scenario, no matter how unlikely it may seem to us, before we rule anything out."

"That's going to be a pretty big list then," Arnie said. "Susie Mae had a way of polarizing people, you know? You either loved her or you hated her, and there wasn't much in between."

"Then we'd better get started right now," I said as I pushed away from the table and stood.

I didn't like where things might lead us, and it could end up straining some relationships that were important to me, but we really didn't have any choice.

We'd agreed to dig into this, and that was exactly what we were going to do, come what may.

Chapter 5

"GET OUT OF TOWN, KILLER!" someone shouted as he drove past us and honked his horn. It was Parker Henson. Had he waited for us to leave to accost us from the safety of his car?

I smiled and waved at him. "Wave to the monkey, boys," I told the men.

"It's going to be like this all of the time if I stay in town, isn't it?" Arnie asked, clearly depressed about the situation. "Is it even worth it?"

"That's entirely up to you," I told him, "but it's been my experience that you can't run away from your problems. Whenever you try, they keep following you around until you deal with them."

"Does that mean that you're starting to think that I'm innocent?" Arnie asked hopefully as I unlocked the front door of Donut Hearts.

I wanted to throw him a bone and tell him that I did, but I couldn't do it, not in good conscience. "It means I'm keeping an open mind. Sorry, I know that's not what you're hoping for, but I'm afraid it's the best I can do right now."

"Hey, I'll take it," he answered, a little more subdued than before.

"The truth is, it's a struggle for me too, Arnie," Phillip admitted as we walked into the shop.

I locked up behind us and wasn't surprised to see that the shop was spotless. Since Emma had dumped her boyfriend, she'd been a demon for cleaning the place. I wasn't sure if she was just trying to be hygienic or if she was washing away some of her troubles, but I wasn't about to complain.

"Take a seat, gentlemen," I told them as I switched on the small coffee pot we kept for ourselves. I didn't always need a large urn of coffee, so it was nice having a smaller option.

"Are you *sure* there aren't any donuts back there?" Arnie asked hopefully.

"There might be one or two. I'll check," I said as I walked into the kitchen. Sure enough, Emma had left a box on my desk holding some misshapen donuts that hadn't made the cut for the displays out front and evidently weren't even good enough to give her classmates. It was my fault they were still there, not my assistant's. I'd boxed them up, meaning to take them to Jake for his trip, when Arnie had walked into the shop.

"How about these? They aren't the prettiest things in the world, but they're tasty," I said, offering the men the box along with small plates and napkins. "If you can wait a few minutes, I'll have some coffee ready for you, too."

Arnie slapped his hands together and rubbed them. "They look amazing to me. When I was growing up, my mom used to say that only five things mattered with the food she served us: taste, taste, taste, taste, and appearance, and the last one didn't count. Her meals weren't always the nicest things to look at, but the woman could surely cook."

"I liked her," Phillip admitted.

"It was probably a blessing she didn't live to see me arrested and convicted of murder, even if I didn't do it," Arnie said.

Phillip and I kept quiet, since there was really nothing that we could say given the situation. I took a napkin and wiped the dry-erase board off, destroying the lettering on the sign to reveal a blank slate.

"Why did you do that?" Phillip asked.

"We need to redo it tomorrow anyway," I told him. I took a marker and wrote across the top, "Suspect. Motive. Means. Opportunity."

"That's a good idea," Phillip said. "Where should we start?"

"I know George and Gabby should be on this list, but I can't bring myself to write their names down," I answered as I pointed the board away from prying eyes outside Donut Hearts.

"Suzanne, we *have* to put everyone up there," Arnie said. "You should start with my name though."

"Is that a confession?" Phillip asked his old friend playfully as he took a bite of an orange-glazed donut that looked more like a C than an O.

"No, but it just makes sense," Arnie said. "Go on, Suzanne. Do it."

I nodded. He was right, after all. "Arnie Lancaster. Money and Love." I paused before filling in responses for the Means and Opportunity. "How exactly was Susie Mae murdered?" I had just realized that I hadn't heard how she'd died yet.

"She was strangled with her scarf from behind," Phillip said.

"It was a scarf I gave her for her birthday. Cost me a fortune, but I thought she'd been worth it at the time."

"Okay, was there anything unusual about *how* she was strangled?" I asked Phillip.

Arnie flinched a little at the question, but I couldn't be delicate about it, not if we were going to really investigate the killing.

"No. I mocked up a punching dummy we had in the basement for the guys to get rid of some stress. It wasn't tough at all to grab the ends of the scarf and pull it enough to strangle her." That was better police work than I'd been expecting from him.

"Could you tell how tall the killer was from the angle of the ligature marks?" I asked.

"Not that we could tell," Phillip answered. "How do you know about those marks?"

"Hey, I've been a cozy mystery lover all of my life. I know things," I told him. "We might as well take off the Means column altogether, since it appears that *anyone* could have done it," I answered as I erased that column.

"Motive and Opportunity should be enough," Phillip said. "Who's next? Suzanne, if you don't want to write their names down, give me the pen, and I'll do it."

"No, I can handle it," I said as I wrote George Morris and Gabby Williams below Arnie's name. For George, I put as Motive: Unrequited

Love, and for Gabby, I wrote Eliminating Competition. "How about Opportunity? Did anyone have an alibi?"

"I sure didn't, and man, I really could have used one," Arnie said.

"We never asked anybody else," Phillip admitted. "I guess we'll just have to ask them now."

I couldn't imagine which would be worse, asking George or Gabby for alibis at the time of the murder. It was sixteen years ago! I had trouble remembering what happened last Thursday, so it might be tough for anyone to have an answer. Then again, they both knew Susie Mae pretty well, so maybe they would remember where they were.

How were we supposed to go about proving it though?

"Who's next?" I asked.

"Our good friend Parker Henson should be up there," Arnie said.

That got Phillip's interest. "Parker? Really?"

"Didn't you know? He grew up next door to Susie Mae. Had a crush on her his entire life. Man, was he upset when she started going out with me," Arnie said.

"I'm sorry," Phillip said. "I missed that."

"Hey, everybody was pressuring you to find an answer fast, and I was the most likely choice by far. I get it," Arnie said with more sympathy for my stepfather than I could have mustered if I'd been in his shoes.

"It's still no excuse for sloppy police work," my stepfather said.

"So we'll get it right this time," Arnie said as he slapped Phillip's shoulder. "If you really want to make it up to me, you'll let me have that last bear claw."

"Really? That's all it's going to take?" Phillip asked as he pushed the box toward his old friend.

"Okay, maybe that's not *all* I need, but it's a good start," he said as he claimed the treat and took a hefty bite. "Man, that's good."

"Glad you like it," I said, always happy to hear praise about my offerings, but the man had been eating prison food for sixteen years, so he wasn't exactly a neutral observer. "Who else makes your list?"

"Maggie Fremont needs to be on it," Arnie said.

"Maggie? Why would the cook's niece subbing at the Boxcar Grill have a reason to kill Susie Mae?" I asked before I'd even written her name down. Hilda was taking an extended vacation to visit her daughter in West Virginia, and she'd gotten Trish to hire her niece, an excellent cook in her own right, to substitute for her. So far, I'd been impressed with the woman's skill in the kitchen.

"The two never did get along. Susie used to babysit Maggie when she was younger, and Maggie hated her for ratting her out to her parents when she caught her sneaking a drink from her dad's bar. She was just fourteen, and man, did they come down hard on her."

"You can't honestly believe that was enough motive for Maggie to kill Susie Mae though," I said.

"I don't know. You remember what it was like as a teenager. You feel everything so much more than you do as an adult. The highs are higher, and the lows are lower. It's possible, that's all I'm saying," Arnie said.

Reluctantly, I wrote Maggie's name along with the others. I hated that three of the four names on my list belonged to varying degrees of friends of mine! I'd known Maggie for a long time. This was turning into a real nightmare.

"Okay, is there anyone else?" I asked them.

"That's all I've got," Arnie admitted. "How about you, Phil?"

"I have a few names we can add to the list," my stepfather said as he dug into the file he'd brought with him. "Let's see. Besides the folks we already have, we need to add Harrick Jackson and Teddy Marcus to the board. I looked into both men at the time, but the leads kind of petered out there at the end."

"Teddy and Harrick? Really? We were all good friends, but I never suspected that either one of them had anything to do with Susie Mae's murder," Arnie said, clearly surprised to hear the other men's names mentioned.

"Yeah, well, maybe they were all a little closer than you realized at the time," Phillip said. "I found out after you'd been in prison for a few years that both men were also seeing Susie Mae on the side, romantically."

"What? No. That's impossible," Arnie said. "The woman was no angel, but Harrick and Teddy? I don't believe it. Who told you that?"

"Harrick himself."

"Why would he even tell you that?" I asked him.

"It was at Teddy's funeral. Harrick had been drinking, and at the wake, he got hammered. He said that he and Teddy both did you dirty behind your back, and he'd regretted it ever since. The man cornered me and told me that you deserved better than you got. When I pushed him about it, he realized who he was talking to and clammed right up."

"What did he mean by that?" Arnie asked. "Was he sorry that he cheated with her or that he killed her?"

"I was never able to get a straight answer out of him," Phillip admitted. "It stuck with me, though, and I've given it some thought over the years."

"So you hadn't written me off completely, even though I was rotting away in prison?" Arnie asked the question, not with malice but with hope.

"No, sir. I suppose deep down, it never sat well with me, even when it was all happening," Phillip finally admitted. "At the time, though, I thought I was doing the right thing."

"I know that, old friend," Arnie said. "Wow, I never would have believed Teddy and Harrick were *both* doing that to me. Some friends they turned out to be."

"It might even be worse than that," I reminded him. "One of them could have taken advantage of your public argument with Susie Mae and killed her to keep her quiet."

"Just to save my feelings from finding out that they'd been fooling around with my girlfriend? I doubt that," Arnie replied.

"What if there were things going on in her life that you had no clue about besides her dalliances? Could she have borrowed money from the other men as well? And why did she need money all of a sudden anyway? What was she up to?"

"I don't guess we'll ever find out," Arnie said, dejectedly.

"That's where you're wrong," I answered. "Folks around town might not like it, but we're going to dig into Susie Mae's past to see if we can't get her some justice."

"You know, the more I think about it, the more I think that we should really start with her sister," Phillip said.

"Lucy? Good luck with that," Arnie said.

"Why do you say that?" I asked.

"That woman hated me from the start," he confessed. "A day didn't go by when she didn't try to talk Susie Mae into dumping me. Remember how she acted at the trial?" Arnie asked Phillip.

Phillip nodded. "She never missed a day, and she sat in the front row, staring daggers at you the entire time."

"The woman actually cheered out loud when they read the verdict," Arnie replied. "How do you think she's going to feel about me showing up on her doorstep? I hate to say it, but maybe I'd better sit that visit out. It's the only way you're going to get anything out of her."

"That's probably for the best," I said. It was a chance for me to discuss a thought I'd been having ever since Momma had volunteered me for the investigation. "Arnie, the truth of the matter is that I'm not so sure that Phillip and I shouldn't handle the entire investigation without you."

"Hang on. I'm not going to just sit by and..."

"Listen to Suzanne for a second," Phillip said as he put a hand on the man's arm to kill his protest. "She makes sense. The second folks see you, they're going to clam up, since most of them have already made up their minds that you did it."

"Gabby Williams didn't seem to think so," Arnie protested.

"When did Gabby *ever* do what anyone expected?" I asked. "We're not cutting you out of the investigation completely. We just need you to stay behind the scenes. If you insist, we can't keep you from coming with us, but if you do, I'm telling you right now, we're never getting to the bottom of this, and in the end, that's really all that counts, isn't it?"

Arnie mulled it over, taking his time to consider what I'd just said. My words had been purposefully harsh, but he'd needed to hear them. "Phil, do you agree with her?" Arnie asked him after nearly a full minute of silence.

"I do," he said. "Like I told you, Suzanne is good at this. We need to trust her instincts."

Wow, suddenly, that was a lot more pressure on me than I'd bargained for, but I knew in my heart that I was right, at least about this.

"Okay then," Arnie said with a sigh. "I'll do what you ask. I guess I've got enough to do around the house to keep me busy for a year, but I'm counting on you both to clear my name."

"I understand you feeling that way, but you need to remember that's not why we're doing this, Arnie. No matter *who* killed her, they deserve to be punished for it, even if we find out it was you all along."

"That's all I can ask," Arnie said. "Is that it, folks?"

"It's all I've got so far," Phillip admitted.

"Then go track down everyone you can find and figure this out," Arnie said as he picked up the now-empty box, the plates, and put our coffee cups in the sink without being asked.

"Just leave those. I can clean up," I told him.

"What can I say? Old habits die hard," he answered with a grin. "I've always been a little obsessed with keeping things neat and clean, and serving time made it even more important to me."

"Well, thanks for doing it," I said as I took a photo of our list with my phone, and then I quickly erased the board. I didn't want any evidence of what we were up to left behind for someone else to see. It wasn't just that I was worried about offending George, Gabby, and Maggie.

I also didn't want the killer to know that we might be on their trail all these years later.

As the three of us walked out of Donut Hearts together, I half expected to see Parker Henson waiting for us to hurl a few more insults our way, but he was nowhere to be found.

That was okay with me. We'd track him down later, but first, we needed to find Lucy, Susie Mae's sister, and see if she might have some thoughts about who else we could talk to about the woman's murder.

If she'd talk to us in the first place.

Chapter 6

AS ARNIE WALKED OFF toward the place he'd inherited from his father, Phillip and I got into my Jeep and drove down Springs Drive.

"Where to, Chief?" I asked him.

"Suzanne, I haven't been the police chief around here in a very long time," he said.

"I meant it more as a figure of speech, not a title," I corrected him. "I've never heard of this Lucy woman. Do you have any idea where she might be, or even her last name?"

"As a matter of fact, I do. We need to go to Union Square," Phillip said.

"So, she stayed close by, but not in town," I said as I headed toward one of our closest sister cities. It was only half an hour away, and I had a great many friends there, including but not limited to the DeAngelis clan of beautiful women who ran Napoli's, my favorite Italian restaurant on the planet.

"As a matter of fact, she runs a nice little business there. Have you ever been to the Crafty Corner?"

"Sure, it's on Main Street near the fire station," I said. "I've been in there a few times. The place is huge. Are you telling me that Susie Mae Long's sister owns it?"

"She does," he said. "She never married, so she still goes by Long too."

"How do you know so much about her?" I asked as I drove.

"I may not be a cop anymore, but I like to keep abreast of things," he said.

"Come on, a craft store though?"

"Hey, I can like to craft too," he protested.

"I know you can. But do you?" I asked him.

"Yeah, I've picked up a new hobby lately. It helps relax me."

This was news to me. "What is it?"

"I'm not so sure it's any of your business," he said, staring out the window.

It was clear my stepfather didn't want to talk about it, but we had a thirty-minute drive ahead of us, and I wasn't afraid to poke a bear from time to time. "You can tell me now, or I can ask Lucy," I told him. "It's your choice."

"I've been crocheting, okay? A lot of men do it," he said a bit defensively.

"I think it's cool," I told him. "I tried it once, but I could never get the hang of it."

When he saw that I wasn't teasing him, he lightened up. "It was tough at first, but I've found that it helps me relax. It takes just enough of my attention to keep me sharp and still let my mind wander about whatever cold case I'm working on. Very therapeutic."

"What does Momma say?"

"She's got me working on a scarf for her right now," Phillip answered with a grin. "I made one for myself, and she liked it so much she asked me to make one for her, too."

"I like scarves," I hinted.

"Okay. Maybe I'll make you one in time for Christmas. I'm not saying which Christmas though," he answered with a smile.

"Hey, as long as I know it's in the pipeline, I'm good with that," I told him. "So, does that mean that you and Lucy are friends?"

"I wouldn't say friends, but she won't lock us out of the store the second we show up, which is what she would have done if Arnie had come with us."

"Are you okay with me benching him during our interrogations?" I asked, afraid that I'd stepped on a few toes doing it.

"Honestly, you saved me the trouble. I knew you were right. I just didn't know how to tell him."

"I don't seem to have a problem with that kind of thing," I admitted.

"That's just one of the reasons I'm happy you're working on this with me," Phillip answered. "In a very real way, this is what I've been doing ever since I retired from the force. This is a cold case, there's no doubt about it. I just hope we're able to get to the bottom of it."

"Even if it looks as though you were right the first time and Arnie really killed her?" I asked softly.

"Even then," he answered without hesitation. "Not knowing is the worst thing. Well, not the worst thing. That would be putting a friend behind bars, even if he was innocent."

I touched his shoulder lightly. "You did the best you could with the information you had at the time," I told him.

"Tell that to Arnie if it turns out that I was wrong," Phillip replied.

"He doesn't seem as though he's holding a grudge," I countered.

"Yeah, that's one of the things that's been bothering me. He had quite the temper before he went away, but I haven't seen any sign of it since he got back."

"Could it be that he was telling the truth, that prison broke him of it?" I asked.

"Absolutely. It's just odd to see, that's all."

We got to the craft store, and I turned to Phillip before we went in. "So, do we lead with our questions about Susie Mae, or do we segue into it gently?"

"You don't know Lucy very well; that's obvious," Phillip answered.

"No, not really. Why do you say that?"

"She considers herself a straight shooter. If we try to dance around what we're doing, and why we're asking her the questions we need to ask her, she's going to have a fit. We might be walking into a buzz saw, but the only way to approach her is head on."

"Hey, I've dealt with Gabby Williams before," I told him, "and nobody ever accused her of being a pussycat."

"Believe it or not, Lucy makes Gabby look like an old softie," Phillip answered as he shook his head briefly.

Oh, boy. That spoke volumes. I took a deep breath, put my hand on the door, and walked right into the lion's den.

I just hoped I made it out alive.

Lucy Long was working on reordering some inventory in the Cricut section, where supplies for the cutting machines stretched practically down a complete aisle. I'd seen some segments on YouTube about the handy little machines, but I had enough on my hands as it was without trying to learn how to use one, no matter how easy they made it look. I'd played with the idea of getting one for Donut Hearts though. Maybe someday. Lucy was a nice-enough-looking woman, certainly no beauty, average in just about every way. Though she wasn't all that much of a beauty, it was clear that she'd kept fit over the years.

Lucy was frowning at the clipboard in her hand when she saw us approach. "Why is it that the numbers in the system never match the inventory I have on hand?"

"Is shoplifting a problem for you?" I asked her.

"My customers don't steal!" Lucy said loudly enough for folks browsing in other sections. "More than once! I have security cameras all over the place."

I saw one older man look around furtively before taking something out of his pocket and putting it back on the shelf.

"Was he actually *stealing* from you?" I asked. "You're taking it pretty calmly."

"That's Wilson Yeats," she told us in a softer voice. "He likes to pretend that he's some kind of bad boy, but he always buys more than he needs, and he overpays for *everything*. He's harmless," she said, dismissing him. "How's the latest scarf coming, Phillip?"

"Slow but sure," he said with a shrug. "My dexterity isn't what it used to be," my stepfather added as he flexed his fingers.

"That's exactly why you need to do this," she said strongly. "It will help you in the long run."

"Yeah, but in the short run, it's killing me," he said with a grin.

"You surely didn't come by for more supplies already, and I doubt your stepdaughter here is looking to take up a hobby," Lucy said. So she knew who I was, which might or might not make questioning her any easier.

"Is this place really all yours?" I asked as I gestured around to the large store. I had to buy supplies for Donut Hearts regularly, and at times, it felt as though I was taking money the customers gave me and handing it over to my suppliers, but it was nowhere near the inventory she must have had on hand.

"I own it all, lock, stock and barrel," she said.

"How did you go about starting it in the first place?" I asked, honestly curious about how someone started a store. Maybe she'd gotten the money in a divorce settlement. That was how I'd gotten the funds to buy Donut Hearts, catching my husband cheating at exactly the right time, just after he'd gotten a big payday for filming a national commercial.

"I got the money as an inheritance," she said. "But I know you're not here to get my life history. Tell me what you want so I can get back to work. I'll warn you though, if you're digging into something that's none of your business, you've come to the wrong place for help." Lucy paused and then added, "Then again, if you're here for advice on where to get started on a new hobby, you're right where you belong."

"I don't have much time for any extracurricular activities, truth be told," I said, ignoring her comment that I was there on an investigation.

"What, between running your donut shop and solving every open case on the books, you don't have blocks of free time on your schedule? You'd be surprised how little time it takes, and how rewarding it can be to see that you've made something that didn't exist before you started."

She was a good saleswoman; I had to give her credit for that. The problem was, though, that she knew that I was an amateur sleuth. As I worked on more and more cases and had more and more luck solving them, my ability to stay under the radar was getting whittled away. Before long, nobody would want to talk to me about an investigation, and when and if that happened, I knew that I'd be through. The main thing I had going for me was the ability to ask questions without being obvious about why I wanted the answers. I'd just have to bite the bullet now and take Phillip's advice and forge ahead into the lion's den.

I really had no choice.

It was time to start grilling her. I was about to do it myself when my stepfather stepped up and did it instead.

"Lucy, we're here because we want to be sure that we got the right guy who killed your sister," Phillip said.

She dropped the clipboard, and her face reddened. "You *arrested* the man who killed her," she said angrily. "The court blew it and let him out, but you did your job."

"I'm not one hundred percent sure of that, truth be told," Phillip said lightly.

"Well, I am!" Lucy snapped.

"Don't you want to be *sure* of it though?" I asked, trying a different approach. "I know people are already saying that he might not have done it after all."

"Is that why you're here, to help him get away with murder?" she asked angrily. "That man killed my sister. Period. End of story."

"All we're doing is looking for the truth," I said. "For Susie Mae."

"You didn't even know her. Why do you care?" Lucy asked, visibly shaken by the reason for our presence.

"Because she deserves justice," I said as calmly as I could. "We figured you might have some insights we don't have about what really happened to her."

"She finally took my advice and dumped the jerk, and he killed her because of it. That's what happened," Lucy said. Her anger was slowly devolving into tears, and I felt like a real heel for opening up an old wound.

"Did you ever think it might be one of the *other* men she was seeing?" Phillip asked her lightly.

"What are you saying, that my sister was some kind of tramp?" Lucy protested.

"We heard that she might have been keeping company with Herrick Jackson and Teddy Marcus at the same time as she was seeing Arnie when she was murdered," I said.

"They were all friends, and that's all they were," she snapped, getting her grief back under control. "You're going to help him get away with it, aren't you?"

"Arnie's free, and nothing we do can put him back behind bars," Phillip said, trying to reason with her, though I was beginning to think that coming there had been hopeless from the beginning, with or without Arnie Lancaster by our side. "Just suppose for a second that he *didn't* do it. What would it hurt to help us dig a little deeper?"

"Regardless, it's too late to do my sister any good," she said angrily. "Now do me a favor and get out of my shop. Now."

There was no doubt in her tone that she was throwing us out, but Phillip didn't move, and neither did I. "Be reasonable, Lucy," Phillip said.

"I said get out!" she said, shouting this time.

"Come on, Phillip. Let's go," I said, knowing that this was a dead end.

"Fine," my stepfather said, but as he turned to go, he said, "If you change your mind, give me a call, Lucy. Susie Mae deserves justice."

"She got it, and then the court took it back," Lucy said as she followed us to the door. "Phillip, you should find someplace else to get your supplies from now on."

He looked genuinely hurt by the banishment. "Come on, Lucy. We're just trying to do the right thing here."

"Not for my sister you aren't," she said loudly. "You can dress it up all you want to, but I know you're helping that killer Arnie Lancaster, and I won't do business with anyone who backs that murdering scumbag."

"That didn't go all that well, did it?" I asked Phillip once we were outside.

"Really? Honestly, it was about what I figured would happen," he told me as we got into the Jeep and headed back to April Springs.

"You were *expecting* that?" I asked him incredulously.

"Pretty much," he admitted.

"Let me get this straight. You *knew* she wouldn't help us, and you even suspected that we'd get thrown out and you'd be banished from shopping at her store, and we went anyway?"

"That's the thing about Lucy," he explained. "She's a hothead. Always been one, always will be. Give her tonight to come to terms with things, and she might turn out to be our best source of information about Susie Mae tomorrow."

"Do you really believe that?" I asked him.

"What choice do I have, Suzanne? We had to try. We did, and whether we failed or not is yet to be seen, but she's not our only subject we need to interview this afternoon."

"I know, but I don't like the idea of talking to many of them, either," I admitted.

"All we can do is what we have to do, and let the chips fall where they may," he answered.

"Maybe, but that doesn't mean I have to like it."

"You? What about me? I've got to find another place to get my yarn now," he said with a grin.

"Unless she has a change of heart about your banishment too," I answered.

"Time will tell, I guess. So, who do you want to tackle next? I know it would be easy to go after Parker and Harrick, but truth be told, I'd like to try to cross some of our friends' names off the list before we go after the others."

"It's not going to make us very popular, but you're probably right," I admitted. "You pick though. Whether we speak with George, Gabby, or Maggie, it's not going to be a very pleasant afternoon."

"Sometimes, that's how it goes," he told me. "At least we have a nice drive back home before we have to upset our friends."

It wasn't long enough though, especially knowing what was ahead of us, but it had to be done nonetheless.

It was just one of the joys of investigating murder in a small town, no matter how long ago the crime may have been committed. Many of our suspects were friends, or at the very least acquaintances.

Murder was retail here, not wholesale, and that made it tougher on everybody involved, even the folks investigating the crime.

Chapter 7

"GABBY, WE NEED TO TALK," I told my friend when Phillip and I walked into her retail shop, ReNEWed.

"Which one of you needs wardrobe advice?" Gabby asked as she sized us both up. She was a trim woman in her late fifties who was always dressed like a socialite. "Strike that. Both of you do. Phillip, I have a few things for men in back, but there's nothing that's going to work for you."

"Hey, what's wrong with what I'm wearing?" he asked as he pointed at his khakis and then his open-collared shirt.

"Do you want the list from top to bottom, or should I hit the highlights randomly?" she asked him with a shrug.

"I'm good, thanks."

"Okay," she said, clearly not agreeing with him. "Suzanne, you I can help. I just got some items in that are a little pricey, but for you, I'll give you my 'friends and family' discount."

"I didn't know you had one of those," I told her.

"I didn't, at least until just now," she answered. "I'm proud of you two for helping Arnie get his life back."

"Actually, that's why we're here, not for a makeover for me." Why did she assume I needed one any more than anyone else? I wore comfortable jeans and T-shirts to work, and while I knew I wasn't setting some kind of style trend in April Springs, I was usually clean and pretty neat. Gabby, and my mother as well, thought I should parade around town in dresses and heels, but that wasn't conducive to my donut shop, or even necessary. Shoot, one of the reasons I loved Donut Hearts was because I didn't have to dress up to go to work.

"Then why are you both in my shop?" she asked.

"It's about Arnie," I said.

"What about him?"

"We're trying to find out what happened to Susie Mae Long," I told her, "and that means digging into the past, even if it's not comfortable for some folks to dredge up bad memories."

"That's just too bad for them," Gabby said roughly.

"I was hoping you'd feel that way," I said.

"Where were you the night Susie Mae was murdered?" Phillip asked baldly.

"What? You expect me to give you an alibi for a night sixteen years ago? Am I a suspect?" She stared hard at us both, waiting for an answer neither one of us wanted to give.

I decided to step in to see if I could calm things down. We'd already dealt with Susie Mae's sister, Lucy, and I didn't want another angry encounter. "Gabby, I know it was a long time ago, but it was a memorable evening for everyone who knew her. All we're trying to do is eliminate people in her circle, okay?"

"Nobody's accusing you of anything," Phillip said, but I swore I could hear a "yet" that he hadn't added. I was going to have to give my stepfather a refresher course in interviewing people without the power of a badge.

"Please?" I asked her, softening my tone. "It would help."

"I'll tell you, but first, I want to know why I'm on the suspect list in the first place," she said, pouting a bit as she spoke.

"We heard you were dating Arnie right before he dumped you for Susie Mae," Phillip said.

"You need to leave my shop, Phillip Martin," Gabby said, barely holding in her anger.

"Come on, it's common knowledge, Gabby. If you didn't do it, you don't have anything to hide."

Gabby stood there for a moment before she turned to me. "Suzanne, is there something wrong with my voice?"

Her question startled me. "No, it sounds fine to me."

"Then why is he still here?"

I shrugged. "Phillip, would you mind waiting outside?"

He was clearly unhappy about being kicked out of two places in less than an hour, but one look at Gabby told him that he'd better not push her any more than he had Lucy.

"I'll be in the Jeep," Phillip said, and without even glancing at Gabby, he left.

"Wow, you were pretty tough on him, weren't you?" I asked her once he was gone.

"I think I handled that perfectly. Feel free to join him on the curb if you disagree."

I wasn't about to budge. It would take more than my friend's considerable bark to get me out of there before she answered our question. "Gabby, it's important we know," I told her. "You do want to help Arnie, don't you?"

"Of course I do. There was a time when he was very important to me," she said, reddening a bit as she said it.

Was it possible that Gabby was still sweet on the man after all these years? I thought about asking her about it, but then I chickened out and decided to keep my focus on the main point of our visit. "Then help us," I said.

"Very well, but just because you asked nicely," she answered. "I was with Teddy Marcus the evening Susie Mae was murdered."

"Wow. I did not see that coming," I told her.

"Get your mind out of the gutter, Suzanne. We were platonic friends; that was all. In fact, he wanted to cry on my shoulder, and back then, I was quite a bit more approachable than I am now."

She would just about have to have been, but I knew better than to say that. "What did he want to talk about?" I asked her.

"Susie Mae, what else?" she asked. "That woman could put a spell on men that was unbelievable, even ones who should have known better. She was a looker, I'll give her that. Long black hair, porcelain-white skin, and the bluest eyes you've ever seen. Put that together with a figure we'd both kill for, and she was formidable."

"I'm guessing you two weren't exactly the best of friends back then," I said, sympathizing with her. Gabby was handsome enough, but no one would ever call her a beauty. They wouldn't call me one either, for that matter, though it was applied to Grace with some regularity. I'd settled long ago for being cute, and Jake found me irresistible, so what anyone else thought didn't matter nearly as much to me.

"No, we weren't all that close," Gabby admitted. "But I still wouldn't want to see her dead."

"Of course you wouldn't," I said. "It's a shame Teddy is dead."

"Yes, it is," she said, and then she looked askance at me. "Suzanne, are you upset because someone died or that I don't have any way of proving my alibi now?"

"Can it be a little bit of both?" I asked her. "I really wanted to strike your name off the list."

"Sorry I couldn't be more accommodating and find you a live witness," she said acidly. "Now, if we're finished here, I've got some new inventory I need to check."

I was being dismissed, and I knew it, but for Gabby, it was practically cordial, especially after the way she'd thrown Phillip out.

"I'll see you later," I told her as I headed for the door.

"You'd be hard-pressed not to, since our shops are side by side," she said in a short manner. I too had overstayed my welcome.

When I got back out to my Jeep, Phillip was grinning like a school kid.

"Did it work?" he asked me when I got in.

"Did what work?"

"Come on. You had to see it. I'm never that ham-handed when it comes to interviewing suspects. I wanted to get her on edge so you could be the sympathetic one after she threw me out."

I had to laugh. "Do you know something? You're smarter than you look," I told him.

"I'd just about have to be, wouldn't I?" he asked with a grin. "What did she say? Does she have an alibi for the evening of the murder?"

"Yes and no," I told him as I made the short drive home.

"What is that supposed to mean, and why are we going to your place?" Phillip asked me.

I ignored one question and answered the other. "I'm not leaving my Jeep in front of Donut Hearts, and our next two suspects are within walking distance. You don't have a problem with that, do you?"

"No. Dot's been trying to get me to exercise more anyway. Did she say something to you?"

"Not today," I told him with a grin.

"Okay. I get it."

As we walked to the park toward city hall, he said, "Come on, don't hold out on me. What does yes and no mean?"

"Her alibi is Teddy Marcus," I told him as we neared the front of the city hall building.

"Who happens to be conveniently deceased," he answered.

"It's not all that convenient for him, but it does make it impossible to prove whether or not she's telling the truth."

"So what are we supposed to do with that?" Phillip asked.

"What we always do. We keep digging."

"George is next, right?"

"Yes. I'm not in any hurry to get thrown out of the Boxcar Grill, so I thought we'd tackle the mayor. He has to at least *try* to be diplomatic with us," I answered, hoping that it was true.

"If you say so," Phillip said.

Before we walked into the building, I hesitated. "Before you try to anger any more of our suspects, give me a heads-up first, okay?"

"It's backfired and bitten me twice in a row," Phillip answered. "I think I'll retire that particular way to question people for now."

"That sounds like a good plan to me," I told him.

We were going to have enough problems with George as it was, and antagonizing him wasn't going to do us any good.

"Well, this can't be good," George said as we walked into his office.

"Nobody was out front, so we came straight in," I told him. "Where's Kath Martin?"

"She's off on some government staffing seminar in Charlotte," he said. "What she's really doing is networking, trying to find a better job, since she finally figured out that she's not getting mine." Kath had been the last in a long line of people working out front as the mayor's secretary, but she was by far the most ambitious of the lot.

"Do you think she'll have any luck?" Phillip asked as he took a seat.

"Knowing her, she'll be tendering her resignation by Monday," he answered.

"You don't seem too torn up about it," I told him as I sat too.

"People come and they go, and there's not much I can do about it, but no, I won't be upset to see the back end of her," George said. "I'm guessing this isn't a social call. Let me take a wild stab at it. You want to know if I killed Susie Mae. Am I right?"

"We don't think you did it," I told him.

"At least not at the moment," Phillip added.

"Are you trying to play bad cop again, despite your promise to drop it?" I asked my stepfather.

"No. George was a good cop. He understands."

The mayor nodded. "As soon as I heard you two were digging into this, I figured you'd be paying a call on me. What took you so long?"

"We had to talk to Lucy first, and then we spoke with Gabby," I replied.

"Woohoo, there's a doubleheader of crabbiness I wouldn't want to tackle on my best day. So, you hit your two hardest interviews first? I've got to say, I admire that."

"Do you know Lucy very well?" I asked him. "She threw us out of her craft shop before we could get more than a few words in. You'd think the fact that we're trying to find her sister's killer would make her want to cooperate with us."

"You might think that, but I wouldn't. They had what you'd call a love/hate relationship the entire time I knew them. One second, they were inseparable, and the next, they were fighting like cats and dogs. Sisters are like that sometimes, I guess."

"So are brothers," Phillip added.

"Family. What are you going to do? You can pick your friends, but you're stuck with the people you're related to. So which one of you is going to work up the nerve to come right out and ask me if I killed her or not? Come on, don't be shy."

"Did you do it?" Phillip asked him earnestly, leaning in as he spoke.

"No, I did not," George said. "That was easy enough. Now, if you'll excuse me, I've got work to do," he added as he gestured to the pile of paperwork on his desk.

"Not so fast, Mr. Mayor," I told him. "You don't happen to have an alibi for the night of the murder, do you?"

"As a matter of fact, I don't," he admitted.

"How about motive? Is it true that you wanted her, but she didn't want you?" I asked.

Phillip said, "Hang on. Take it easy, Suzanne."

"It's a fair question," I said, "and I expect an answer."

George stared at me for a few minutes and then did something that surprised me. He laughed. "Good for you. Wow, you really do have some stones, there, lady."

"You didn't answer the question," I told him.

"Sure, I had reason enough, I guess. I told her she was wasting her time on Arnie and that I was a better man in just about every way she could figure, but she plain wasn't interested. I might have been a broke cop making peanuts, but I was a good guy, and that should have counted for something. When I realized that I wasn't what she wanted, I wrote her off and moved on." He looked as though the memory still upset him, even all these years later.

"You're still a good guy," I told him. "Did Arnie have much money?" I hadn't heard about that angle yet, but it was an intriguing thought.

"Everybody in town thought so. He always talked a big game back then," the mayor said. He turned to Phillip and asked, "Do you remember the roll of ones he used to carry around in his pocket? It was big enough to choke a horse."

"I don't care how many he had, that wouldn't be enough to impress anyone," I countered.

"It would if all you saw was the hundred-dollar bill on the outside of the roll," Phillip explained. "Yeah, I remember. Take it easy though, George. He was a friend of mine back then."

"And now?" the mayor asked him.

"I'm not sure yet," my stepfather admitted.

George shrugged. "You're entitled to your opinion, even if you're wrong. He killed her, and it's going to take a lot to convince me otherwise. I'd watch him pretty carefully if I were the two of you. I think he's using you both."

"Why do you think that?"

"He wants to come back home," George said, "but he can't do that with this cloud hanging over his head. If he can get a former police chief and one of the most influential private citizens in town on his side, there's half the battle right there."

"Who is he recruiting besides Phillip?" I asked in perfect innocence.

"He's talking about you, Suzanne," my stepfather said with a slight smile.

"George, you need to get out more. If I'm one of the most influential folks in April Springs, things are going downhill fast." The very idea of it shocked me to my core. Sure, I knew a great many folks liked me, or more importantly, my donuts, but I was hardly a mover and a shaker.

"Don't sell yourself short, Suzanne," George said.

I'd had about as much of that nonsense as I cared to hear. "What if you're wrong about him, George? Aren't you willing to admit that it's at least possible that Arnie didn't kill Susie Mae?"

"One percent, maybe two," he said grudgingly.

"Okay, it's not much, but I'll take it. Who would you look at if you were trying to solve this case yourself?" I asked him.

"I wouldn't," George said flatly. "It would be a waste of time. I'm sorry, but we caught the man who killed Susie Mae, and how they could let him off like that is beyond the scope of my imagination. Sorry I don't have a clean alibi for you. I guess I'll have to stay on the list."

"For now," I agreed. "You seem pretty calm about it."

"That's because I know I didn't do it," George said. "I wasn't kidding about this work. I need to get back to it. I'd wish you luck, but you're both on a fool's errand that's not going anywhere. He did it. Period."

I stood, realizing that the mayor wasn't going to give us anything else. "Come on, Phillip. We have a few more folks to speak with this afternoon."

"Who else are you going after?" George asked me.

"I'm not sure it should matter to you, since you've already made up your mind," I told him with a smile to take the sting out of my comment.

"Point taken," he said dismissively as Phillip and I left.

As we walked over to the Boxcar Grill, I told Phillip, "Something just occurred to me. Arnie said that he didn't have an alibi the night of the murder, right?"

"That's true," Phillip said. "Why do you ask?"

"What if he had one, but he was protecting someone?" I asked.

"You're just grasping at straws now, Suzanne. You could say the same thing about George if that's the case."

I hadn't considered it, but it was a valid idea. "You're right."

"Hold on, I was just trying to make a point," Phillip protested.

"I know that, but it could be true nonetheless. Is there anyone George might try to protect by withholding their name?"

Phillip just shrugged. "After all this time? I can't imagine who it would be."

"Let's keep it in mind though, and we should ask Arnie again when we see him later." It wasn't many steps from city hall to the Boxcar Grill, so I stopped and took a deep breath before I mounted the steps. "Are you ready for this?"

"Yeah, but I'm sure hoping I don't get banned from the Boxcar like I did from Lucy's shop. I can find another place to get stuff for my crocheting, but I'd have a hard time finding another place to eat, especially if Dot's out of town like she is right now."

"Then maybe we should both be extra polite when we talk to Maggie," I told him.

"I will if you will," he answered with a slight smile.

"Done and done," I said as I finally got up the nerve to walk up the steps and ask Maggie for her alibi, something I had a feeling she was going to be none too happy about.

Chapter 8

"TWICE IN ONE DAY," Trish said as we walked back into the Boxcar Grill. "Wow, I feel special. How desperate are the two of you, anyway? Jake and Dot go away, and suddenly, you're both living in my back pocket."

"As good as your food is, why wouldn't we hang around here?" I added, "We'd love to chat with Maggie for a second."

"Sorry, but you'll have to get in line," Trish said, frowning suddenly.

"She's not here?" Phillip asked.

"The woman took off out the back the second Arnie Lancaster walked in the front door with you. I had to call Gladys in to cover for her, and you know how she hates to be the lone cook." Gladys Murphy was good, but she was certainly no Hilda, or Maggie either, for that matter.

"I'm sorry if we caused you any trouble," I said as I motioned for Phillip to leave. "We'll catch up with her later."

"Hang on one second, you two. Why do you want to talk to Maggie? I told Hilda I'd look out for her while she was here."

"Susie Mae used to babysit her," I offered, hoping that would be enough. "We were hoping to get some insights into her life just before she died." That was true. It just wasn't all of the truth.

"She hated her, I know that much," Trish said softly.

"You knew about that?" I asked.

"She confided in me what happened the other night when we were working late. Can you imagine how guilty she must have felt?"

"Why would she feel guilty?" Phillip asked, leaning forward a bit.

"How would *you* feel? Maggie told Susie Mae she wished she would die, and the next thing she hears is that it actually happened. She feels like she was responsible for what happened even to this day," Trish explained. "Do me a favor and don't bring it up to her, would you?"

"I'm sorry. I truly wish we could do that, but we really need to speak with her," I told my dear friend.

Trish's face turned ashen. "Are you kidding me? Do you think she actually had something to do with what happened to that poor woman?"

"We don't know," Phillip said. "That's what we're trying to find out."

Trish shook her head and scowled. "Honestly, I'm not surprised you'd push her like that, Phillip, but Suzanne, I have to say that I'm disappointed in you."

Her words stung, I couldn't lie, but there wasn't much I could do about it. "Don't you think it would be better if the questions came from a friend?"

"I do. Do you happen to know where I can find one?"

Wow, I was really taking some hits here. "Sorry we bothered you," I said. I wanted to get out of there before either one of us said something we couldn't take back later.

"So am I," Trish said.

We were at the bottom step when Trish flew out the door. "Suzanne. Hang on a second."

"Why, do you want to get a few more shots in before I go?" I asked her.

"I'm sorry, okay? That was uncalled for. It's just with Maggie leaving suddenly and Gladys panicking in the kitchen, I'm about on my last nerve. You just picked the exact wrong time to come by and ask questions. I didn't mean it, all right? I really am sorry. You know me and my big mouth. Sometimes, it has a mind of its own."

"Yeah, I have that problem sometimes myself," I said.

"Are we okay?" Trish asked.

"Sure," I answered.

"Okay, now this time, say it like you mean it," Trish pushed.

"We're fine," I said as I fought back a smile. "I won't do anything to upset her if I can help it, but whether we like it or not, she was a part of this way back when. Trust me, it hasn't been a joy for Phillip and me. We've already aggravated the woman's sister, Gabby, George, and now you. If I didn't have to investigate more tonight, I'd go home, take a long, hot shower, and call it a night, but we've got two more folks to talk to before I can do that."

"I don't get it; I admit it. Why are you both doing this in the first place? Phillip, you put him away, but as far as I know, you don't have any connections to the case at all, Suzanne."

"Momma asked me to help him," I said simply.

"Okay, *now* I understand," she answered.

I knew that would be all it would take. Trish understood my relationship with my mother just about better than anyone else, except maybe for Grace. Even Jake and Phillip had a tough time with it sometimes. "Mothers and daughters, right?"

"Right," she said. "I'd love to chat more, but Gladys is probably setting the place on fire in panic."

"We won't keep you then," I told her.

Trish started back up the steps but stopped at the top. "Are you sure we're good?"

"As gold," I told her.

"That's a relief. I'd hate to have to go out looking for more friends," she answered with a smile.

"How do you think I feel? We're alienating most of the ones I've got."

"Don't worry, we'll all still love you when all is said and done," she said.

"How about me?" Phillip asked, trying to be playful.

"*You* we're still not sure about," Trish answered, and then she laughed as she went back inside.

"She didn't mean that, did she?" Phillip asked once the Boxcar owner was gone.

"Of course not," I reassured him. "She wouldn't tease you if she didn't like you."

"Then she must love you beyond all comprehension," he told me.

"Yeah, I get that a lot. Should we try to track Maggie down now, or should we find Parker Henson and Harrick Jackson?"

"You said you'd like to go home and get some rest," Phillip answered. "We could always take it up again in the morning."

"I'm working at Donut Hearts tomorrow," I reminded him. "We can't get started until eleven, so we'd better do what we can tonight."

"Okay," Phillip said. "At least our suspects are close by."

"We hope," I said. "They all live in town, but that doesn't mean they're home."

"There's only one way to find out, isn't there?"

"I'm ready if you are," I said, sad that Trish and I had a dustup but happy that it was already over. It was nice to have that kind of friend, one that might anger quickly but was just as ready to apologize. I wished all my friends were like that, but I'd take what I could get.

"Come on. Seriously?" Parker Henson said when he answered his door and found us there. "I'm entitled to my opinion. The last time I checked, America was still the land of the free."

"We're not here to talk about your behavior earlier," I told him.

"Good, because I'm not going to listen to a lecture I didn't sign up for. Why you'd side with that killer is beyond me. He did it. You know it, Chief," Parker said as he turned to my stepfather. "You arrested him in the first place. What happened? Are you getting soft in your old age?"

I thought Phillip might react to the goading, but he just smiled. "In some ways, maybe I am. But in others, not so much. I don't have the constraints that I used to have as a police officer now. It's amazing the kind of things I can get away with as a private citizen."

"Is that a threat?" Parker asked heatedly. "You heard him. He just threatened me."

"I heard no such thing," I said. I couldn't even blame Phillip for poking the man, at least verbally. As long as my stepfather didn't follow through, he'd be fine. It appeared that Phillip was trying to rattle the man, and from where I stood, it was working. "You're not exactly an innocent bystander here, are you?"

"I don't know what you're talking about," Parker said. "I just hate seeing somebody get away with murder. He's the *only* one who could have killed her."

"That's not true at all," Phillip said calmly. His even demeanor seemed to shake Parker up more than he would have if he'd been more aggressive, which I was sure was my stepfather's plan all along.

"Did Arnie tell you that? Come on, get real. If that man told me it was raining, I'd have to poke my head out the window to be sure."

"So, are you saying that you *didn't* grow up next door to Susie Mae?" I asked him.

"Yeah. So what?"

"We heard you had a massive crush on her," Phillip said. "When she started dating Arnie, you lost it and threatened him. What happened, Parker? Did she turn you down, and that made you angry enough to kill her?"

"What? No! Of course not! That's ridiculous!"

Wow, this guy sure had a temper. Arnie's theory about Parker's possible involvement in the murder was starting to look more plausible by the second.

"You had a crush on her though," Phillip said calmly.

"Sure I did, but so did most of the guys in town," he admitted. "I dated Lucy for a while to try to get Susie Mae to see me as a real option, but she figured out what I was doing pretty fast."

"Susie Mae or Lucy?" I asked.

"Yes to both," he answered with a shrug. "I didn't mean to hurt Lucy, but when Susie Mae was around, she kind of faded into the background, you know?"

I'd met the woman, and I was pretty sure she wouldn't take being dumped very well. "How did Lucy react when you dropped her?" I asked.

"Honestly, she was kind of used to it. I wasn't the first guy who tried to get close to her sister through her."

"Let's get back to Susie Mae," Phillip prodded. "You were angry with her when she wouldn't dump Arnie for you. Come on, at least admit that much."

"Sure, I was upset, but I wouldn't have touched a hair on Susie Mae's head. Now if *Arnie* had turned up dead back then, I belonged on the suspect list, but I wouldn't be by myself, you know what I mean?"

I had a sudden thought. "Did you frame him for the murder, Parker? Is that why you're so upset that he's out now? Do you think he's going to get payback for what you did?"

"I didn't have to frame him," Parker said, now really starting to boil. "He did it!"

"Tell you what," Phillip said. "Give us an alibi, and we'll leave you alone."

"From sixteen years ago? You're kidding, right?"

I prodded him a bit. "Come on, Parker. It was a tragic night. If you were so smitten by Susie Mae, you'd remember where you were the night she was murdered."

He shrugged. "I was home, by myself," he answered. "Lucy came over and knocked on my door, and I figured she was trying to get back together with me, but when she told me the news, she was a real mess, crying and carrying on something awful, which is about what you'd expect, given the fact that her sister had just been murdered. I didn't believe her at first, but after a minute, it started to sink in. That's when I went looking for Arnie Lancaster."

"You what?" Phillip asked.

"I was going to kill him for what he'd done," Parker said. "I probably shouldn't tell an ex-cop that, but it's the truth. It was lucky for both of us that I didn't find him, or I might have just done it."

"Wow, you really do still hate him, don't you?" I asked softly.

"He took away the only woman I ever really loved," Parker said with a shrug. "Is it any wonder I feel the way I do?"

"But she didn't love you back," I pointed out gently.

"No, but while she was still alive, there was hope for me, and that rat dog stole it from me."

There was a question I wanted to ask, and I figured there was no better time. "Do you still want to kill Arnie, Parker?"

"No, not anymore. I'm not happy about him being free and all, but he's not worth throwing my life away for. I figure he'll get his in the end, but it won't be by my hand. Listen, I really don't want to talk about this anymore."

He started to go back inside when Phillip asked, "Are you going to keep hounding Arnie like you've been doing?"

Parker shook his head as he ran his hands through his hair. "No, I'm done with the man. As far as I'm concerned, he died when Susie Mae did, and it doesn't make sense to let a dead man bother me anymore. I'm going to leave the past right where it belongs, in my rearview mirror."

"One more thing," I asked before he closed the door. "Did she sleep with you too, Parker? And did you loan her any money?"

"That's two things, but the answer's the same for both questions. It's none of your business," Parker answered with some real heat before he slammed the door in our faces.

"Do you believe him?" I asked Phillip once we were on our way to Harrick's address.

"Which part?"

"All of it. Any of it. I don't know," I answered. It wasn't the most illuminating response I could give the question, but it was the truth.

"I've always had a hard time reading him; I readily admit that," Phillip said. "If he had an alibi, I'd like it a lot more, but I did hear about him dating Lucy just before Susie Mae was murdered. I didn't figure it mattered all that much, given what happened."

"I don't see how it could. I was just curious, that's all."

"I'm not willing to strike his name off our list of suspects because of what he told us a minute ago," Phillip said. "I wouldn't mind asking Lucy about it, just to get her take on things."

"Are you honestly thinking about going back and interviewing her again after that disaster this afternoon?" I asked.

"Like I said before, she should calm down by tomorrow."

"If you say so," I told him as we got to Harrick Jackson's place. "Wow, this is never easy, is it?"

"If it were, everyone would do it," Phillip answered with a slight smile.

"Phillip. Suzanne. What brings you by? I was just going out for a bite," Harrick said, even though it was late to be eating, especially by my standards. Harrick had clearly been a handsome man in his youth, and age hadn't robbed him of his looks. He was trim, sported neat gray hair cut short, and he wore nicer clothes than anyone else I knew, with the possible exception of Gabby, though I doubted any of his had been gently used by anyone else.

"Where are you headed?" I asked.

"I'm meeting a young lady in Union Square," he admitted.

"How young is she?" I asked on a whim.

He looked annoyed with me, which I didn't mind. It was my turn to poke the bear, and I could see why Phillip enjoyed doing it so much. It was fun.

"She's old enough to date me," he said. "What can I do for you?"

"We're here about Susie Mae Long," Phillip told him.

The man stiffened a bit at the mention of the dead woman's name. "What about her? She's been gone so long it's almost as though she were never here."

"She was though, Harrick, and somebody killed her," Phillip replied.

"We all know it was Arnie Lancaster," Harrick replied icily. "To think we were friends! It still galls me thinking about it."

"Were you sleeping with her, Harrick?" Phillip asked nonchalantly.

"She wasn't exclusive with Arnie, despite what people thought," he answered.

"I take it that's a yes," I said.

Harrick waved a hand in the air, as though he could dismiss us so easily.

"Did you loan her money?" I followed up.

"She was in a bit of a jam, so I loaned her a few dollars," he said. "I knew she would repay me, so it wasn't a big deal."

"Did she though?" Phillip asked.

"She didn't live long enough to manage it," he answered. "Honestly, why are you asking me these questions?"

"We'd love to ask you one more. Do you have an alibi for the night of the murder?"

"I do," he answered.

"Care to share it with us?" Phillip asked.

"Not particularly. She's a formidable woman, and I have no desire to get on her bad side. Phillip, you are no longer with the police, and Suzanne, you are just a donutmaker. I see no need to answer any more of your questions."

That got Phillip's ire up. "First of all, Suzanne is so many more things than a donutmaker that you're showing your ignorance by saying so."

It was sweet of him to defend me, but I was a big girl, and I could handle this man myself. "What you say may be true, that we have no status in the case, but do you honestly believe that the current chief of police wouldn't be interested in what we have to say? You're going to answer these questions one way or the other. We just thought it would be easier if you told us instead of having the police come by at midnight to grill you."

That last bit I'd added for drama's sake, but it didn't do any good. "Let them come at midnight. I'm afraid I won't be here though. My dates tend to run into the next morning. Now, if you'll excuse me, I don't want to keep the lady waiting."

"Who were you with, Harrick?" I asked him one last time, but he just smiled, got into his car, and drove away.

"Wow, that guy has a real set on him, doesn't he?" Phillip asked me.

"You didn't have to defend me, as sweet as it was," I told him.

"I wanted to. Sorry if I overstepped my bounds, but it bugs the fool out of me when people underestimate you."

"Is that the former police chief talking or my current stepfather?" I asked him with a slight grin.

"The latter," he admitted. "We're family, Suzanne, and I won't stand by while someone treats you badly."

"Thanks. I appreciate that," I said. "What about Harrick? Do you have any idea who this mystery lady was who might provide him with an alibi?"

"I do, but I'm confused," Phillip admitted.

"I'm listening. Why don't you tell me, and we'll see if we can prove it, one way or the other?"

"You're going to think I'm crazy, and I know she gave us someone else as an alibi, but I think he might have been talking about Gabby Williams."

Chapter 9

"GABBY? WHY WOULD SHE lie to us about her alibi if she had someone alive who could verify she was telling us the truth about not being involved in Susie Mae's murder?"

"You know her better than I do," Phillip answered. "You tell me."

"I'm baffled by it," I said. I glanced at my watch. It was still early for most folks, but for a donutmaker, it was way past my bedtime. "We need to ask her in the morning," I added as I stifled a yawn. "I hate to be a party pooper, but three o'clock tomorrow morning is going to be here before I know it."

"I'm amazed you lasted as long as you did. We didn't even stop for dinner."

"Believe it or not, I'm not even all that hungry," I said as my stomach rumbled.

"Tell you what. You go home and get something to eat before you go to bed, and I'll go by Arnie's and bring him up to speed on what we've been up to."

I'd forgotten all about my promise to keep Arnie Lancaster posted on our progress. "No, it's okay. I'll go with you."

"Suzanne, I can handle this. You need your rest."

"I'll be fine," I said. I'd promised both Momma and Jake I'd watch Phillip's back, so there was no way I was letting him go to Arnie's place alone. "We can stand here arguing about it for another half hour, or we can drive over to Arnie's place so we can call it a night. It's your choice."

"Drive," he said as we got into my Jeep and headed over to Arnie's house.

"You might as well stop pounding. He's clearly not here," I said after the fourth time we knocked on the front door.

"I don't like this, Suzanne," Phillip said as he knocked loudly again.

"I'm not keen on it either, but there's no way we can *make* him stay home," I replied.

Phillip started to leave, at least that was what I thought he was doing, but instead of heading back to the Jeep, he started to walk around the house, peeking into windows.

"You know, there's a law against being a Peeping Tom," I told him.

"I'm worried something happened to him."

Phillip's concern was getting to me, too. Had something happened to the man so soon after being freed from prison? Had someone decided that if the courts wouldn't take care of him, they'd do it themselves? The world had gotten crazier and crazier lately, and it wouldn't have surprised me if that was exactly what occurred.

When we got to the back, there was still no sign of life, but we did attract the attention of his neighbor, an elderly man who decided to become the Neighborhood Watch group all by himself. "Take off! I'm calling the cops on you prowlers," he said as he grabbed his phone.

"Mr. Pierce, it's me, Phillip Martin," Phillip said as he walked over so the man could get a closer look at him. The irony of Mr. Pierce being the neighborhood watch was that the man was nearly blind, but that didn't stop him from going after someone he thought was a bad guy.

"Chief Martin? Is that you?" he asked.

"It is. I'm with Dot's girl, Suzanne."

I hadn't been a girl in donkey years, but I understood why my stepfather had referred to me that way. In a great many people's minds in April Springs, I could become the president of the United States, and they would still think of me as Dot's girl. That was one of the downsides of small-town living they didn't mention in the cozy mysteries I loved to read.

"The donut girl?" he asked, squinting at me carefully.

"One and the same, Mr. Pierce," I said. "Have you seen Arnie Lancaster?"

"Of course I've seen him. The boy grew up next door to me. He mowed my lawn when he was a kid. What a question."

"I mean tonight," I clarified. "Have you seen him tonight?"

"I surely have. He hightailed it out of here an hour ago like his tail was on fire. I called out to him, but he just waved and kept on hustling down the street. You know," he told Phillip sternly, "you did a lot of good when you were the chief of police, but you got that one wrong. That boy didn't kill that girl, and we both know it."

"We're looking into it," he told him, trying to get back up front. It was no easy matter, at least not without Mr. Pierce following us.

"Better late than never, huh?" he asked.

"Did you know Susie Mae?" I asked him. The older gent might have some insights that hadn't occurred to us, and besides, what would it hurt to ask?

"Both those girls were bad news," he said with a frown.

"Both of what girls?" Phillip asked.

"Susie Mae and Lucy both, sisters always up to no good. One time on Halloween, I caught them splitting an entire bowl of my candy between them when they didn't think I was home. I was there all right, watching the little beggars and seeing who I could trust and who I couldn't." He looked at me and smiled. "You and Gracie always took one apiece. You were good girls," he added.

"That's what the sign said to do," I told him, never knowing that he'd been watching us from the other side of the door.

"And you abided by the law, unlike what you and that step-pappy of yours are doing now. Trespassing is trespassing, people. Now, I'll let you go this time, but let's not let it happen again, do you hear?"

I wasn't sure if he was planning on making a citizen's arrest of a former police chief and a donutmaker, but the guy was spunky enough to try it.

"We'll be good," I told him as we got back to my Jeep and drove off, waving as we left.

"I can't believe he's still alive. That man was ancient when I was a pup," Phillip said, "though thinking back on it, he's probably only twenty-five or thirty years older than I am."

"That's still pretty old," I said with a grin.

"Hey, watch it, young lady," Phillip replied.

"Yes, sir, I will. Where do you think Arnie went?"

"I wish I knew," Phillip said, "but it doesn't make any sense driving around April Springs looking for him."

I stifled a yawn. "I'm game if you are."

"You need to get something to eat and then get to bed," he told me. "It's way past your bedtime, and you know it."

"Wow, you're sounding more and more like a stepfather every day," I told him.

"I'm just thinking about how your mother would feel about me keeping you out late," he said awkwardly.

"She wouldn't be pleased," I agreed.

"No, she would not."

As I drove him back to their cottage, I said, "I need to ask you something before I drop you off, and I want you to think long and hard about your answer before you speak."

That certainly got his attention, which was my plan. "Go on."

"I need you to promise me you won't investigate this case without me," I answered.

"Do you mean tonight?"

"I mean while we're working together. You're not the only one who has to answer to my mother, and if something happens to you on my watch, I'm going to be in for a world of hurt."

"Yeah, I get that," he said. "Okay, I promise."

"I'm serious, Phillip," I insisted, wanting to be sure he wasn't just making an idle pledge he planned on breaking the moment I was gone.

"I hear you. I want to go back over my files from the case anyway, so I'll work on them tonight and then again tomorrow while you're working. You close at eleven, right?"

"Yes, but I'll need fifteen minutes to get everything in order after that," I answered. "Make it eleven fifteen, and I should be ready to start digging again."

We got to the cottage, but he hesitated before getting out. "Since we're being all serious and everything, I've got something to ask you."

"Go ahead, I'm listening," I told him.

"Any chance you're making cherry fritters in the morning? With your mother away, I would surely love three or four of those without getting into trouble for eating them."

"How about if I make you one?" I countered.

"Come on, make it at least two," he said.

"Okay, two, but no more, no matter how much you beg for more," I told him with a grin. "I don't usually make those this time of year, but for you, I'll make an exception."

"I appreciate that," Phillip said as he finally got out of the Jeep.

"Should I wait here until I'm sure you get inside safely?" I asked him.

He laughed, but it was totally devoid of humor. "Oh, you're serious? Suzanne Hart, I'm a grown man, a former chief of police, and an all-around armed tough hombre to boot. You don't have to worry about me."

"What can I say? It goes with the territory," I told him.

"What territory is that?"

"Family," I answered simply.

His frown faded and was slowly replaced by a slight grin. "Yeah, I like that. I'll be careful if you promise to do the same."

"You have my word. I'm going home, grabbing a quick bite and an even quicker shower, and then I'm headed for the hay. See you tomorrow."

"And you won't forget, will you?"

"The fritters? I'll try to remember," I told him, and then I broke out a bright smile. "Of course I won't forget. See you tomorrow. Sleep well."

"You too," he said.

As I drove home, I wondered what Jake was up to, and to my delight, my phone rang, and it was the man himself. "We must have ESPN or something. I was just thinking of you," I told him.

"That joke never gets old, Suzanne. Is this a bad time?"

"No, it's perfect. I'm heading home from Phillip's, so I'd love to chat. How's it going there?"

"My dear, sweet, misguided sister has fallen in love again," Jake said ominously.

"Oh, no. Do we not like him?" My sister-in-law, Sarah, had a bad picker when it came to the men in her life, and she was a constant source of worry for my husband.

"That's the problem. We do. At least I do," Jake admitted.

"And that's a problem why exactly?"

"I don't know. I can't put my finger on it, but there's something there," Jake replied.

"Are you doing a background check on him?" I asked.

"Suzanne, I'm not that bad, am I?"

"You didn't answer the question, sir," I reminded him.

"I've got a buddy looking into him," he finally admitted. "No red flags yet, but he's just started digging."

"Wow, sometimes paranoia can get the best of you, Jake. Maybe she finally got herself a good guy. It would be a nice change of pace."

"Yeah, maybe. How are you doing?"

"Well, let me tell you, Phillip and I are making friends wherever we go. So far today, we've managed to aggravate the victim's sister, our mayor, Gabby Williams, and Trish."

"Trish? Why Trish?"

"We brought Arnie to the Boxcar Grill for lunch, and the second Maggie saw him, she took off out the back door. It seems she had a history with Susie Mae, and seeing Arnie out and about brought up a lot of bad memories for her."

"You know you can't make everyone happy when you dig into murder," Jake reminded me.

"I get that, but I hate alienating my friends," I said as I drove up to the cottage, dark and empty with my husband so far away.

"Have you alienated anyone who's *not* your friend?" he asked as I shut off the Jeep and walked up onto the front porch. The owl who'd taken up residence in our woods hooted his greeting to me, and if I hadn't been on the phone with Jake, I probably would have hooted back like I usually did.

"A couple of people," I admitted when I saw something that didn't belong. "Jake, I need to call you back."

He had to have heard something in my voice. "Suzanne, what is it? Call Chief Grant right now!"

"It's nothing," I said, though that was a lie.

"Suzanne, if you don't talk to me this instant, I'm leaving Raleigh and heading back to April Springs."

"It appears that someone has tucked a *Get Out Of Jail Free* card from an old Monopoly game in our door," I said. "That's not a threat, Jake, it's a comment." Still, I pulled the card out with my handkerchief and flipped it over. On the back of it, printed in block letters, it said, "STOP DIGGING." I decided not to share that bit with my husband. "I told you we upset some folks here. Someone's just showing their displeasure in a pretty passive-aggressive way."

"Maybe. Do me a favor and go inside, would you?"

"Sure," I said as I unlocked the door and walked in, locking it behind me.

"Is it dead-bolted?" he asked.

"Yes, but don't let that paranoia of yours rub off on me. It's harmless, Jake."

"So you say, but I'm calling Chief Grant, so hang up and stay by the door."

"Jake, it's not necessary," I insisted.

"Suzanne, this is not up for negotiation. Either you let me call him, or I'm coming home."

"Make the call, but you're being silly," I told him.

"I can live with that," he replied.

As I waited for the police chief, I thought about digging out our own Monopoly set and substituting one of our cards for the one I held in my hand, but I decided that would be pushing it a bit too far, especially if it turned out to be important. I did the next best thing, though, and pulled out my phone. After taking several shots of the front and back of the card, I was just finishing up when I heard someone outside.

Chief Grant had arrived on my doorstep in three minutes. "That was a record, even for you," I said as I let him in.

"Jake called, I came," he explained. As he held out a plastic evidence bag, he said, "Let me have it, Suzanne."

"You mean please, right?" I asked him, holding on to it tightly.

"Yes, please," he amended.

"That's the spirit," I said as I placed it in the offered bag.

"Did you happen to mention the warning on the back to Jake?" he asked me after flipping the bag over.

"What do you think? Chief, you know as well as I do that I've ruffled quite a few feathers today, and don't act like you aren't aware of it. I know your grapevine is better than mine."

"That would be tough, given that your customers keep you in the loop constantly," he said.

"Don't downplay the connections you've made over the years as police chief," I answered. "This is just someone's idea of a joke."

"Well, if it is, it's not funny."

"Okay, not necessarily a joke, but it's nothing to take too seriously. We don't need to tell Jake about this, do we?" He was about to speak when I added, "Before you say anything, you should know that Jake is visiting his sister, and he's worried about her." All of that was true. There wasn't a time when my husband wasn't worried about Sarah, and if I'd made it sound a bit more dire than it really was, I was just going to have to live with it.

"I suppose I can keep this between us for now," he said as he tucked the bagged card into his pocket. I was about to thank him when he said, "On one condition."

"Stephen Grant, I gave my mother my word I would help Phillip dig into this case, and I'm not about to break it."

"Take a breath, Suzanne. That wasn't what I was going to ask you."

I didn't believe him, but I was still willing to hear what he had to say.

"Go on, then. I'm listening."

"If anything else happens, and I mean anything, you tell me, and then you tell your husband, and I mean all of it," he said gravely.

"He's not going to be very happy you're keeping things from him. You know that, right?" I reminded him.

"I'll deal with that when and if it comes up. You and I have been friends a long time. I'm willing to cut you a little slack if you make me that promise."

I didn't see any other way out of it that wouldn't bring my husband racing home. "Okay, I suppose you've got a point. I agree."

He was about to say something more, and then he changed his mind and bit it back down. Good for him. I'd given him my word, and that was going to have to be enough. "Now, may I please get something to eat and get some sleep?" I asked him. "I've got a big day tomorrow."

"Catching a killer?" he asked.

"Making donuts. Phillip has requested cherry fritters, and that's going to take a little more time than I'm used to."

"Cherry fritters?" he asked as his face lit up. "I *love* your cherry fritters."

I had to laugh. "Fine, I'll make a few extra for you, too."

"That's all I'm asking," he answered with a grin. "Have a good night."

"You too," I told him.

After he was gone, I thought about that game card and who might have hand-delivered it to my cottage. Chances were it wasn't anything significant, but just in case, I slept upstairs in my old bedroom. It wasn't that it was any safer than the one I now shared with my husband on the first floor, but I got a sense of comfort there that was hard to explain.

I wasn't sure I'd be able to get to sleep after eating some leftover pizza I nuked and a small salad to go with it. Okay, I had a few cookies for dessert, too, but hey, a girl deserves a treat every now and then, or what's the point of living? I slept soundly after a quick shower, but my alarm jarred me awake much sooner than I was ready for.

It was another day of donutmaking and crime solving.

No wonder I stayed tired all of the time.

Chapter 10

I HALF EXPECTED TO find another Monopoly card on my doorstep at Donut Hearts when I unlocked the front door, but there was nothing there out of the ordinary. I guess they got their point across with one.

Either that, or they'd run out of cards.

I flipped on a light, the coffee pot, and the oil, in that order. As I started mixing the batter for the cake donuts, the first order of my day, I wondered again who had left me the unusual calling card. Honestly, it could have been any one of the multitude of folks we'd grilled the day before. It appeared that our list of suspects had one thing in common: they wanted the past to stay buried in the past.

Unfortunately, for them anyway, that wasn't going to happen. As I separated the large bowl of batter into smaller containers so I could flavor the batches individually, I wondered where Arnie had gone last night and if he'd ever come home. How about Maggie? Was she going to be absent from the Boxcar Grill today, or would she show up so we could speak with her? I didn't think she killed Susie Mae, but running away like that didn't look good. Then again, George, Gabby, Lucy, Parker, and Harrick hadn't exactly welcomed our questions with open arms.

As I started dropping the batter into the hot oil for the old-fashioned donuts—usually my first donut made of the day—I tried to focus on the oil and not the case we were working on. This stuff was boiling hot, and it would do some serious damage if I got sloppy around it and burned myself. In my job, there were times I could ponder the secrets of the universe and other instances where I had to pay attention or suffer the consequences.

"Good morning, Suzanne," Emma said when she came into the shop right on time. "How goes the world of donutmaking this morning?"

"Different day, same old stuff," I told her with a grin. "How's life treating you?"

"I can't complain," she answered as she grabbed her apron and started in on the dishes I'd already built up for her.

"If you did, no one would listen anyway, right?" I asked with a laugh.

"You would," she countered.

"That's true," I agreed. "So, how was class with Jason Clover?"

She actually blushed a bit. "He actually carried my books to my car after class. How old-fashioned can you get?"

"I don't know. I think it's kind of sweet," I said.

"Don't tell him, but I think so too," Emma answered with a hint of laughter in her voice. "Before you ask, I'm still getting over the breakup, so I'm not ready to start dating again."

"But when you do, how high is Jason going to be on your list?"

She shrugged. "At the moment, he's at the top of it."

"He's a good-looking guy, isn't he?" I asked with a grin.

"Suzanne, you're a happily married woman. You're not supposed to notice those things."

"Emma, I'm married; I'm not dead. It's okay. Jake wouldn't mind me saying it."

"How is your husband doing? How long is he going to be in Raleigh?"

"Are you trying to change the subject, young lady?" I asked her with a smile.

"That depends. Is it working?"

I had to laugh. "Okay, I get the message. I'll drop it."

"Finally," she replied with a huge smile, and then we were both laughing. We didn't necessarily make a lot of money at the donut shop, but we sure had fun.

Later that shift, at the start of our break we took every morning between the batter donuts and the yeast ones, Emma said, "There's something you need to know about, Suzanne."

"Why do I not like the sound of that?"

"Dad is running a special edition of the paper today." Emma's father, Ray Blake, was a journalist of questionable ethics and even more uncertain talent who ran a weekly ad flyer as though he thought it was the *New York Times*.

"I don't even have to ask what the subject matter is, do I?"

"I'm sure you can guess. I grabbed a copy for you, but don't tell him you got a sneak peek," she said as she withdrew a thin newspaper from her oversized handbag and handed it to me.

"Thanks. I think," I said as I read the headline. In large bold letters across the top, it screamed, "MURDER IN APRIL SPRINGS' PAST." He'd run a headshot of the deceased in garish color, and I marveled at what a beautiful woman Susie Mae Long had been. No wonder she'd had so many suitors. Compared to her sister, Lucy was a pale imitation, and I doubted that she'd ever been able to hold a candle to her sister's looks. The article was Ray's style all the way, casting suspicion on several of the folks we were looking at now, though Arnie was clearly center stage.

"Where does he get his information?" I asked, surprised that, for a change of pace, Ray had actually gotten close to a few motives Phillip and I had uncovered.

"He's got his sources," Emma said, "but he won't tell anyone who they are."

"Not even you?" I asked her.

"Not even Mom," she countered. "Besides, we don't talk about his stories anymore, not after he almost ruined our friendship with you."

I'd been tough on Ray for his past behavior, but I hated the thought of being the one who had caused trouble in their home. "I don't know. Maybe I was a little too hard on him," I admitted.

"Honestly, I don't think you were hard enough," Emma said. "Anyway, I thought you should see this. I hope it doesn't mess up your investigation."

"You know about that?" I asked her.

"*Everybody* knows about it," she answered. "Dad even knows, but at least he didn't print that part. I suppose that's something, anyway."

"I suppose it is," I replied. "Who knows? Maybe this will help."

"How can that be true?"

"Well, it might just make the real killer jumpy, and we can take advantage of that."

Emma frowned. "I thought everyone believed that Arnie did it. Are you thinking Chief Martin got it wrong back then?"

"We're trying to keep open minds," I admitted. "Arnie certainly wasn't the *only* person in April Springs who had a beef with Susie Mae."

"Okay, stop right there. Don't tell me anything else. I'd hate to be tempted to tell Dad anything that might even hint at me betraying your confidences."

A little later in the morning, Emma asked, "Are those *cherry* fritters you're making?" as I dropped a batch into the hot oil.

"I had a special request, so I figured I'd knock some out," I told her. "Why, do you want me to save one for you?"

"No, they're too sweet for my taste. I'll take apple anytime," she replied. "Who's getting the royal treatment?"

"A former chief of police of ours, as well as the current one," I said as I flipped them all over so both sides could get equally done.

"So it's a lawman thing," she said with a grin.

"Not necessarily. Jake likes apple better too, just like you do."

"I knew I liked that man for a reason," she said with a laugh.

"I'm kind of fond of him myself," I told her as I pulled the finished fritters out and put them on the rack to ice. After I had eight made, I started on the apple fritters. I had some customers who insisted on them, and who was I to disappoint my fans?

When I opened the shop at six a.m., per my custom every day, I was surprised to find someone waiting for me, a patron who had never been in Donut Hearts before, at least to my knowledge.

"Lucy Long, I'm surprised to see you here so bright and early," I said as I unlocked the door and let her in.

"I just had to come by and apologize for my behavior yesterday," Lucy said, her face a bit flushed. "I'm embarrassed about it, and I hope you'll forgive me. Your questions just brought up a lot of bad memories for me, ones I've tried for the past sixteen years to put behind me."

"I understand, and I'm sorry we had to ask," I told her, feeling some sympathy for the woman and forgiving her for her earlier reaction. I was an only child, but Grace had been more like a sister to me than some siblings ever were. If anything happened to her, I would still be feeling the pain of my loss sixteen years later, so it just made sense that Lucy was still hurting from the murder, no matter how long ago it might have been.

"It's okay. I talked to a few friends, and they convinced me that I should cooperate with you both. Is Phillip here by any chance?" she asked as she looked around the empty shop.

"No, right now, it's just Emma and me," I said as my assistant poked her head out of the kitchen, started to say something, and then waved as she ducked back in.

"Well, I'll just have to tell him myself later," she said. "If there's anything I can do, don't hesitate to ask. I'll be at the craft store all day."

"I didn't think Phillip was allowed there anymore," I told her gently.

"Wow, I really was a jerk, wasn't I?" she asked as she looked embarrassed by the memory. "I'll call him and invite him myself."

"That's okay, I'll tell him, and we'll stop by later this afternoon, if that's okay with you."

"It's fine. Have you made any progress on the case?"

Of course she'd want to know where things stood. I just wished that I had something to tell her. "It's slow going. Sixteen years is a long time, but we're going to do our best to jog some folks' memories. Were you able to come up with anything that might be helpful?"

"Actually, I made you a list," she said and handed me a folded piece of paper.

I unfolded it and read the names she'd listed. It was no surprise that Arnie was on top, but it also included George, Parker, and Harrick.

"These are all men," I told her, surprised she hadn't included Gabby or Maggie.

She just shrugged. "That's all I could come up with. Does it help at all?"

"As a matter of fact, it does. We're looking at all of them," I told her, withholding the fact that this wasn't our complete list of suspects.

"Well, I hope you find whoever killed my sister," she answered as she glanced at the donuts on display behind me. "Suzanne, would it be too much trouble for you to box up a few dozen of your favorites for me? I'd like to offer them to my customers today."

"It's no trouble at all," I told her. "After all, this is a donut shop," I added with a grin.

I had been about to offer them to her on the house, given what had gone on before, but I wasn't going to be able to pay my bills giving donuts away, especially not ones I still had a chance to sell. Fortunately, she was more than willing to pay for them, so after I gave her the change due her, I handed her the boxes.

"Thanks for coming all the way to April Springs to set things right," I told her.

"After the way I behaved yesterday, it was the least I could do." The woman really was quite reasonable once she got over the surprise of being grilled about her late sister's life. As she left, I realized that I had to give Phillip credit. He'd predicted this very thing. Sometimes it was difficult for me to remember that my stepfather had been a pretty good police officer once upon a time.

"Hello, Chief," I told the police chief when he walked into Donut Hearts a little later that morning.

I had his bag of cherry fritters waiting for him at the cash register. As he paid me, he took the offered bag, opened it, and then took a big whiff. The smile on his face said it all.

"Before you start counting, there are only two in there."

"Come on, Suzanne. Two is hardly worth the trouble of eating."

I reached to retrieve the bag, but he was too quick for me. "I don't want you experiencing any hardships on my account."

"I'll suffer through," he said with a grin. "Let's keep this between us, okay? Grace doesn't need to know what I'm eating while she's gone."

"I don't know. She *is* my best friend," I told him with a smile.

"Hey, we're helping each other out here, remember? Have you heard from Jake this morning?"

He was clearly pointing out that he'd kept silent about something for me, and he expected a little quid pro quo. "No, not yet, but I get the message. Unless she asks me a direct question, I won't say a word."

"Is that the best you can do?" he asked me.

"Sorry, but it is."

"That's okay. I'll take it." Chief Grant lowered his voice as he asked, "Has anything happened since last night?"

"A great deal has happened since then," I told him jokingly. "You'll have to be more specific."

"You know what I'm talking about," he said, not rising to the bait.

"There haven't been any more messages or warnings or even errant game cards left on my doorstep. It's been a pretty quiet morning, at least so far."

"Good. That's what I like to hear," he said.

"Did you come by here for the fritters or because you were worried about me?" I asked him.

"Yes," he replied with a slight smile. Shaking the bag in my direction and grinning, he added, "Have a good day."

"Right back at you," I told him.

It was nice of the police chief to check up on me, but I knew if anything happened to me while Jake was away, he'd have been in a world of serious hurt. Besides, we'd been friends for a long time, and it didn't hurt that his wife was like my sister. I pretty much had every bit of his protection that I was willing to accept, which wasn't a whole lot. Just because his intentions were good didn't mean that I needed babysitting. That word, babysitting, made me think of Maggie, and I had to wonder if she'd returned to the Boxcar Grill or if her absence was ongoing. I considered giving Trish a call, but I figured it would be better if Phillip and I popped over there for lunch. That way, we could get a bite to eat and snoop around at the same time, a win-win in my book any day.

Chapter 11

I WAS JUST CLOSING Donut Hearts for the day when I saw Phillip rush up to the door. After I held the door for him, I said, "You didn't have to hurry. I would have unlocked the place for you."

"I know, but I wanted to see if I could beat you to the punch." Sometimes men were just grown-up boys, even ones as old as my stepfather. He took a deep breath. "I smell fritters. Cherry fritters, to be precise."

"It is impossible to tell whether I made them or not this morning, given all of the different aromas in this shop at the end of the day."

He frowned a bit. "You made them though, right? Please tell me you didn't forget."

"I didn't forget," I said to him. "Do me a favor so I can at least look my mother in the eye when she asks me if I fed you any treats while she was gone. Eat half of one now and save the rest for later when I'm not around."

"I can try, but I'm not making any promises," he told me, the sparkle in his eyes twinkling ever so brightly.

"Okay, if you can't show restraint, I'll have to do it for you." I took out the box I'd put aside for him, the one loaded with three cherry fritters, and took one out. He looked happy as I plated it but not so much when he watched me cut it in half and put part of it back in with its friends.

"Half? Seriously? Is it even worth eating such a small piece?"

I smiled as I picked up the half still on his plate and put it back with the rest. "That's your call, my friend."

"On second thought, half sound great," he told me hurriedly. "Please?"

I couldn't resist. I retrieved the half and put it back on the plate. "Would you like some coffee to go with that?"

"Actually, milk sounds even better," he said. "You know me; I like it cold."

"Coming right up."

After I served him, he looked toward the kitchen. "Is it safe to talk?" Phillip asked me softly.

"It should be. I let Emma go half an hour ago," I said just as quietly.

"Excellent," he said as he took a bite.

"Are you talking about our privacy or that fritter?"

"Can't it be both?" he asked as a customer I didn't recognize knocked on the door.

"Sorry, we're closed," I told him after I walked over.

"Then why is *he* eating? Come on. I'll make it worth your while. It's an emergency. I drove all the way from Maple Hollow. Please?"

I couldn't turn him down, especially after seeing how sad he looked.

"Fine," I said as I turned to Phillip. "Hold that thought."

I opened the door, and he looked at the empty trays on display. Again, his face fell. "Aw, man, I'm too late anyway."

"Not necessarily. How do you have a donut emergency, anyway?"

"You know how cravings can be," he said.

"As a matter of fact, I do," I told him as I brought out five boxes, brimming with leftover donuts from the day's sales. It was tough to judge how many I'd need on any given day, but I always tried to err on the side of having too many rather than not enough. "Tell me what you like, and I'll try to find them for you."

"You're kidding, right? I'll take 'em all!"

"You don't have to feel obligated to buy me out just because I let you in the door," I told him.

"Suzanne, you made a sale. Stop trying to talk the man out of it," Phillip answered before turning to the man. "Am I right, or am I right?"

"You may just be my new best friend," the man said with a smile as he offered his hand. "I'm Kirby. Nice to meet you."

"Nice to meet you, sir. I'm Phillip."

"If you two boys are finished getting to know each other, that will be twenty-five dollars, please."

"I'm sorry if you misunderstood me," the man said, looking puzzled. "I said I wanted them all."

"And that's what I'm selling you. You can have them half off, since my workday is now officially over."

I thought I was doing him a favor, but he just shook his head as he pulled out three twenties. "There you go."

"This is way too much," I protested.

"Respectfully, it's just right. That will cover the donuts, and a thank-you tip for opening up for me after you were already closed."

"Take his money before he tastes one and tries to double it," Phillip advised me. "All you need to do is put the cash in the till and say thank you."

I knew better than to try to argue with both of them. "Thank you," I said.

Kirby grinned at me and then slapped Phillip on the back. "Phil, old buddy, I believe we are brothers from different mothers."

"Let me get the door for you, Kirby," he said with a chuckle.

Once Kirby was gone, I said, "Wow, you make friends easily, don't you?"

"Hey, what can I say? We bonded over donuts. I can think of worse starts to friendships than that," he replied. "Do you turn down money as a habit, or was that just a moment of weakness?"

"I was just going to donate them or even throw them away," I admitted. "I feel as though I robbed that poor man."

Phillip put his hands over what was left of his fritter. "Hush now, you'll frighten him."

I smiled, and then I said, "Enough about donuts. Boy, do I have a lot to tell you."

"I'm listening," he said as he finished off his half fritter and started looking longingly at the box that held its mate.

"Fine. You can have the other half, but if you don't have any appetite for lunch, it's on you," I said as I retrieved the other half and put it on his plate.

"I guarantee you that's not going to happen," my stepfather said with a smile as he took another bite. "Go on. I can eat and listen at the same time."

"Fine. First off, last night when I got home, I found a calling card tucked into the frame of my front door."

"What happened? Did you miss a door-to-door salesman while we were out crime-solving?" he asked, clearly euphoric about getting more fritter.

"It wasn't that kind of card," I said. I pulled out my phone and scrolled to the photos I'd taken the night before, happy that I'd had time to snap them before the chief had shown up to confiscate the evidence.

Phillip took it from me and frowned when he saw the game card. When he swiped to the next shot and read the message, he got really agitated, so much that he pushed the plate holding the last bit of fritter away from himself. "You got this, and you didn't call me immediately? Suzanne, you can't take chances like that! I should have known about this the second you found it."

"What could you have done if I'd called, Phillip?" I asked him.

"I would have rushed right over, that's what. After I looked the place over, I would have slept on your couch and kept watch over the cottage, but I couldn't do any of that, because you didn't call me." He seemed genuinely upset about it.

"First of all, I was on the phone with Jake when I found it, and second, he called Chief Grant, who came over in less time than it takes to tell you about it. Why are all of you so worried about me? I'm getting kind of tired of dealing with a bunch of overprotective men."

"Sorry, but that's the price you pay for being loved," he said gruffly. "What did Jake say about the note?" I hesitated answering, and before

I could say anything, he added, "You didn't tell him, did you? Seriously?"

"He would have just rushed home, even though it was nothing," I explained.

"And Chief Grant went along with that?"

"He wasn't happy about it, but he agreed we'd keep it between us," I admitted.

"Wow, I'm surprised he'd take a chance incurring Jake's wrath like that," Phillip answered.

"Maybe because it was just somebody trying to scare us off," I said. "Doesn't that usually mean that we're getting close to something they don't want us to find out?"

He conceded the point. "Maybe, but I still don't like it."

"I'm not thrilled about it, either," I said, "but we need to take it as a good sign and keep digging even harder."

I looked over to find Phillip smiling as I ran the report for my cash register. "What's so funny?"

"Funny? Nothing. I'm just impressed. I love seeing you dig in your heels like this. You're a bit of a pit bull, aren't you?"

"Those dogs aren't necessarily bad, just the folks who train them to be," I told him.

"Tell that to the chunk of my rear end one got a hold of when I tried to serve an eviction notice back in the day," he said as he gingerly rubbed his backside. "Then again, the owner had a pretty good bark and bite on her, too, so maybe you've got a point. What I'm trying to say is that I admire your willingness to keep going in spite of being threatened to back off."

"In spite of? Try 'because of,'" I told him. "Anyway, that was just one thing that happened. Do you want to hear the rest of it?" I asked as I finished counting the money on hand and totaled it on a slip of paper so I could compare it to the report that was still running. I knew I should upgrade my cash register to a newer model, but it was good enough for now, and I wasn't exactly floating in extra cash at the moment.

"I'm all ears," he said as he finished his fritter.

"You can beg all you want to, but you're not getting the rest until this evening," I said, putting the box on a shelf out of his reach at the moment.

"Spoilsport," he said. "Go on, finish bringing me up to speed."

"Okay. Check this out," I said as I grabbed the early-edition newspaper Emma had given me earlier.

Phillip whistled as he read the headline. "Wow, it didn't take him long to put that out, did it?"

"In his defense, it's a pretty big story."

"Are you actually *defending* the man?" Phillip asked me in wonder. He knew the troubled history I had with Ray Blake, so I couldn't actually blame him for being surprised. Truth was I was a bit startled myself.

"Hey, that is what he does," I said, brushing off the question. "Go on, read it and tell me what you think."

Phillip studied the paper and then set it aside. "He got some of it right, some is just pure conjecture on his part, and the rest of it is somewhere in between."

"What do you think about how it might impact our investigation?" I asked, which had really been my question.

"I think it could only help," Phillip said. "This will just get our suspects on edge, even if they aren't mentioned, directly or otherwise."

Ray had skirted using actual names in his story, instead painting them as anonymous suspects, even though it wouldn't be that difficult figuring out exactly who he was talking about. No one had successfully sued him yet, and I had a hunch Ray would welcome a trial if it ever came to that. The attention alone would be worth it to him, as well as the notoriety of him being able to claim he was just defending the freedom of the press to anyone who would stop and listen.

"What do you think?"

"I agree with you. We can use this to turn the heat up on the folks we talk to today," I answered as I checked my totals. I was off exactly sixty dollars, and it took me a second to realize that I hadn't rung in Kirby's after-hours sale. That gave me a perfect balance, so I filled out the deposit slip and got ready for the next part of my closing duties, wiping the tables down and sweeping the floors.

"How long do you think you will be?" he asked.

"It will go quicker if you grab a broom," I told him.

I'd been teasing him, but to my surprise, he took my broom and started sweeping.

"Hey, I was kidding!"

"I wasn't," he said with a grin. "I'm not above working for my food."

"Good, but you need to wipe the tables down first," I said as I traded the broom for a clean dishrag. "There's an order to these things."

"I'm here to learn," he said with a smile. Apparently, cherry fritters were the way to a man's heart, at least a former, or even current, chief of police. "What else do you have?"

"You were right about something yesterday," I told him as I got busy with some of my other tasks.

"Don't sound so surprised," he said. After a moment, he added, "Right about what in particular?"

"Lucy came by to see me, and she couldn't have been nicer if she'd tried," I admitted.

"Told you so," Phillip said with a smile.

"Hey, there's no need to gloat. We've been invited to come by the craft store later this afternoon. Even you. She's decided to lift your lifetime ban."

"Thank goodness," Phillip said. "That's good news. Lucy might be able to give us some insights into her sister's life at the end."

"Hopefully she can do just that," I said.

"Is that it?" Phillip asked as he put the rag on the counter and took up the broom again.

"I thought that was a lot," I told him.

"It was," he assured me. "Now, do you want to know what *I've* been up to?"

I stopped and looked hard at him. "I thought we agreed you weren't going to do any investigating unless we were together. I was under the impression I'd made myself clear last night, but apparently that wasn't the case."

"Take it easy, Suzanne. I did what I promised you I'd do. I dug into the old files and the newspaper stories at the time and tried to look at the case again with a fresh perspective, and that's it. You've been a lot more active than I ever dreamed about being, so if anyone needs to apologize, it's you."

"I was just running my donut shop," I said, defending myself. "How does that make anything I learned my fault?"

"It doesn't," he said, giving in instantly. "Now, do you want to waste a little more time arguing about something that didn't happen, or would you like to know what I found out?"

"I'll let it go for the moment, but I reserve the right to argue later," I told him with a smile. "But for now, I'd love to know what you discovered."

"That's the thing. So would I," Phillip said as he frowned.

Chapter 12

"OKAY, YOU'RE GOING to have to explain what you mean," I told him.

"As I dug deeper and deeper into everything, I kept getting the feeling that I was missing something," he admitted. "I kept going over everything time and time again, but whatever it was vanished as quickly as it had appeared. Something is in that stack of papers, but I can't for the life of me figure out what it was or what it could mean. Maybe I'm losing my touch in my old age."

"I seriously doubt that," I said. "If anything, you're a better investigator now than you ever were when you were the chief of police."

He seemed surprised by the praise. "Do you really think so?"

"I do," I told him earnestly. "Don't force yourself to try to remember, or you'll never figure out what caught your attention in the first place. Sleep on it, or at the very least try to let it go for now and see if you have any better idea about what it was later."

"I suppose that's really all I can do," he admitted. "Are we finished here?"

I loved how closing Donut Hearts had gone from my job to ours, but I wasn't about to say anything. "We are," I said as I started flipping the rest of the lights off. "After we swing by the bank, we need to go over to the Boxcar Grill."

"Yeah, I'm still a little hungry," he said as he patted his stomach lightly.

I refrained from commenting on the large fritter he'd just eaten. "We can eat, but that's not the main reason I want to go over there. We need to see if Maggie is back on the job, and if so, why she took off like a spooked rabbit like she did yesterday."

"Hey, I love multitasking, as long as one of those tasks is eating at the Boxcar," he said. "So what are we waiting for? Let's go!"

Unfortunately, that wasn't meant to be.

As I was locking the front door behind us, I heard someone calling out to us from across the street.

It was Arnie Lancaster.

He'd been on my list before, but suddenly, he had managed to move himself right up to the top.

It was time to find out what kind of game he was playing.

"Where have you been?" I asked him before Phillip could beat me to it.

"Around," he said nonchalantly. "I didn't realize you were looking for me."

"Arnie, get inside," Phillip said roughly.

"She just locked the door, so it's going to be a little tough."

If he thought he was funny, he was wrong.

I unlocked the door, and we all went back into Donut Hearts.

"I could sure use a donut," he said as he looked around.

"Sorry, but we're sold out," I told him.

"Come on. All of them? Not even a misfit or two like you gave us yesterday? You can't find one in back for good old Arnie?"

The guy's smugness was getting on my nerves. "I said I was sold out, and I meant just that. You stood us up."

"I didn't realize we had plans this morning," Arnie protested.

"She's talking about last night, Arnie," Phillip said. "We came by your place to bring you up to speed on what we'd done, but you weren't there."

"I must have been asleep," he said as his eyes kept darting around the shop.

"We know you left the premises," Phillip pushed.

"Premises? Now you sound like a cop again," Arnie replied.

"Suzanne, I don't know about you, but I've had about enough of this guy. Are you ready to call it quits?"

"I'm with you," I said as I unlocked the door again. "Come on, Arnie. We're leaving."

"Hey, don't be so sensitive," he complained. "I had somewhere I needed to be. Is that okay with you?"

"That depends on where you were," I answered.

"I wasn't doing anything illegal if that's what you're asking," Arnie replied, not really answering at all.

"I'm finished," I said. "Now, are you going to leave willingly, or am I going to have to throw you out? It's your call."

"Are you *threatening* me?" Arnie asked me.

"Don't kid yourself. She can handle better men than you, but she won't have to. I'm good at taking out the trash." He put a hand on Arnie's shoulder and squeezed hard enough to make the man flinch.

"Take it easy, there, Phil. That hurts."

"Good. It's meant to. And by the way, it's Phillip. Do you understand?" my stepfather asked with that commanding presence he had sometimes. Jake had the Voice too, and so did Stephen. It must have come from being in charge and expecting people to listen to you, and none of the men needed badges to make themselves heard.

"Got it. Phillip, would you please let go of me so I can tell you what I was doing?"

"I'm sorry. Didn't you hear us earlier? We're finished with you and your case, Arnie."

"I was tailing Harrick Johnson, okay? That's why I was gone when you came by the house. He's the one who killed Susie Mae, and I was trying to get some proof to convince you of it."

"What makes you think Harrick did it?" I asked as Phillip eased up on his grip. "And don't try to tell us it's something in your gut. We need evidence."

"How about this?" Arnie asked as he pulled a faded old letter from his pocket.

"Where did you get that?" Phillip asked.

"It was mixed in with all of my old things," Arnie explained. "My pop collected all of my stuff when I got sent away, and this letter was tucked in the back of an old book Susie Mae gave me a few weeks before she died. I didn't think about it again until I was sorting through everything and stumbled across it. Go on. Read it."

I started to take the letter, but Phillip handed me a pair of gloves from his pocket. Arnie protested, "Don't bother. It's got my prints all over it."

"I know that, but it might have someone else's fingerprints on it, too," Phillip said.

"I never thought about that," Arnie said.

After I put on the clear neoprene gloves, I pulled the letter out and read it aloud.

Susie Mae,

You've lost your mind if you think I'm going to let you blackmail me. I'm warning you, if you try to use what you've got on me, I'll ruin you! Don't try to pet a snake; it will bite you every time.

Harry

"Who's Harry?" I asked.

"It was Susie Mae's nickname for Harrick," Arnie explained. "The only person he'd ever use that name with was her."

"Why did she give it to you?" Phillip asked.

"I had no idea," Arnie said. "She did that sometimes. Susie Mae would ask me to hold onto something for her, and I did it every time. The truth is that she loved writing notes and getting them in return. It was like she was some kind of schoolgirl passing things in class. A lot of times, it was the only way you could ever get a straight answer out of her. We all did it with her. It was the easiest way to make her happy."

"And you thought of telling me this *now*?" Phillip asked him as I walked back to my office to make a quick copy of the note. When I got back, Phillip protested, "Why didn't you tell me about all of that after I arrested you?"

"Let's face it," Arnie said with a snort. "Even if I'd known that particular letter was there and I'd showed it to you, by then, you were already convinced that I did it. The truth is that I didn't remember anything about it until I saw it again last night. I had a few other things on my mind back then if you'll recall."

"It doesn't prove anything," I said as I studied it a little more carefully.

"What, you don't think it's real?" Arnie asked indignantly. "I'm a lot of things, but I'm not a liar, Suzanne." He then turned to Phillip. "Tell her, Phil...lip." He'd almost blown it, but he managed to recover just in time.

"You were usually pretty truthful," Phillip agreed. "So, do you think this is proof Harrick killed her?"

"You don't?" Arnie asked, clearly upset.

"I think it means that he merits a closer look, but it's no excuse to go off on your own and try to prove anything," Phillip told him. "Suzanne and I are working on the case, so you have to be patient."

Apparently, we were still investigating, at least according to my partner, and as long as he was in, I was too.

"I got antsy," he admitted.

"Then take up a hobby. If you say you're going to be somewhere, be there. You get one more chance, Arnie. Stay out of this, and let us do what we do best."

"Does that mean you're not giving up on me?" Arnie asked earnestly.

"For the moment," I answered for both of us.

"I'll take it. So, should we go talk to Harrick now or what? If we sweat him, I know that we can get the truth out of him."

"*You're* going home," Phillip said. "Suzanne and I will speak to him about this, but we have a few other things we have to deal with first."

"But..."

I cut him off. "Go home, Arnie."

"Fine," he said grumpily. "Just prove he did it so I can start my life over, will you?"

"Like we said before," Phillip replied, "we're looking for evidence pointing to who really killed Susie Mae. Whoever that might be."

I let us all out, and Arnie took off, hopefully toward his place. As Phillip and I walked across Springs Drive to the Boxcar Grill, I asked, "Is this note legit?"

"I honestly don't know. It looks like Harrick's handwriting," Phillip admitted.

"How could you possibly know that?"

"I read his deposition last night. He signed it, and the H is pretty distinctive," Phillip explained. "It isn't a perfect match, but then most signatures aren't. That's where a lot of forgers go wrong. They copy something identically without any variation."

"Should we go talk to Harrick now?" I asked.

"He's on our list, but first, I'm getting something to eat," Phillip answered.

"And we need to talk to Maggie if she's there," I reminded him.

"That too."

Trish didn't look all that happy to see us, which was a bad sign. "She didn't come in today, did she?" I asked with trepidation.

"Oh, she's back there all right, but I wouldn't order today's special if I were you. The gal's definitely off her game."

"I'm so sorry," I told Trish. "We won't bother her."

"That's where you're wrong," she told us both. "You're going back there right now and straightening this mess out once and for all."

"We can't promise anything," I told her.

"You can promise me one thing," Trish insisted.

"What's that?"

"That you'll at least try."

"We promise," I said.

I took a deep breath, and then we walked back into the kitchen, usually a place I felt most comfortable in, but suddenly I wanted to be just about anywhere else, and one look at Phillip's face told me that he felt the exact same way.

"Hey, Suzanne, Phillip." Maggie looked haggard, though she was younger than me, and if she'd gotten four hours of sleep the night before, I would have been amazed.

"Hi," we answered in near unison.

Maggie glanced at Phillip overtly. "I don't mean anything by this, but would you mind if I spoke with Suzanne alone?"

"That's fine with me," Phillip said, almost relieved as he backed out of the kitchen before I could grab his arm and stop him.

"You should know that I'm going to tell him anything and everything we discuss, so we might as well bring him back in," I told Maggie. Phillip had stood up for me too many times for me not to return the favor.

"I can't. Not in front of him. Please?"

She looked as though she wanted to cry. I was torn. Should I do what she wanted and risk offending my stepfather, or should I bring him back in, thus killing her willingness to talk to either one of us? I decided to make my apologies to Phillip later. The case came first, and he knew that better than just about anybody else.

"Fine. Why did you run away yesterday?"

"You know why," she said as she refused to make eye contact with me.

"Arnie Lancaster," I said flatly.

"Yes," she admitted.

"Maggie, we've already heard the whole story," I told her.

"Who told you?" she asked, and then she knew it. "Arnie did, didn't he? Susie Mae told him everything, so naturally, he told you."

"It's not that big a deal," I told her. "You were young, and we've all done stupid things when we were that age."

"I didn't kill her, Suzanne!" Maggie protested so loudly that I expected Trish to burst through the door at any second.

"I'm talking about her catching you sneaking a drink of your dad's liquor," I told her. "She told your folks, didn't she?"

"Yes, and I made things even worse by telling her I wished she were dead," Maggie said, breaking down from the memory of it, even so many years later.

Maggie came to me and wrapped her arms around me, sobbing the entire time. Trish poked her head through the door, but the second she saw us there, she pulled her head back in.

After a few moments, the substitute cook pulled back. "Sorry about that. I still get upset thinking about what happened."

"Why wouldn't you? It's only human."

"You don't really think I killed her, do you?" Maggie asked me as she dabbed at her tears.

"I'm not the one you have to convince," I told her, ducking her direct question. "If you had an alibi, it would be different, but..."

"I do though. Didn't Arnie tell you that part? Or does he even know?"

"What's your alibi, Maggie?" I asked her.

"I was at my aunt's house."

"Hilda is your alibi?" I asked.

"No, Aunt Hilda is my mom's sister. I'm talking about my dad's sister. My folks sent me there as my punishment for sneaking that drink. I had to stay with her all week, and my banishment started the second Susie Mae told my folks what I'd done!"

"I didn't know you had another aunt around here," I said.

"She's in Hickory. Ask her. Go on, she'll tell you I was there. She couldn't stop talking about Susie Mae's murder, like she was famous or something."

Maggie pulled out her phone and made a call. I listened carefully for any clue that she might have set this alibi up ahead of time. She said,

"Hey, Aunt Jenny. I know. I'm sorry. It has been a while. Listen, I've got a friend here who wants to ask you a question. Just tell her the truth, no matter what, okay? I'll call you back later and tell you all about it. Just do this, please?"

She thrust her phone toward me, and I took it.

"Hello, Jenny. I need to know if you can confirm the presence of your niece in your home sixteen years ago when a woman from April Springs was murdered."

"She was with me, all right, the little sneaking drunk. Stealing booze from her old man! I couldn't believe it. Her father was no prize, but he deserved better than her for a kid. He drove her straight here to my place, and I didn't take my eyes off her for one second for the entire week. What's this all about?"

"We're trying to put together what really happened," I said as evasively as possible.

"Well, she didn't do it, I can tell you that much. The way that girl carried on though, crying and screaming and crying some more, you'd have thought she'd just lost kin, not some babysitter." In a more telling tone, she asked, "So the police are digging into that murder, are you? Who do you think did it?"

"I'm sorry, but I'm not at liberty to discuss the case at this moment," I said as officially as I could sound.

I never claimed to be a cop, and if she assumed that I was one, that was on her, not me.

"Fine. Be that way. Put my no-good niece back on the line."

"I'm sorry, but she's aiding us in our investigation, so she can't talk right now." Then I hung up on her.

Maggie was grinning when I turned back to her. "I've been wanting to do that since I learned how to use a telephone," she said with a broad smile. "Did she back me up?"

"She did," I said. It wasn't the tightest of alibis, but I had a feeling that Jenny wouldn't lie to save her niece's skin, so I had a hunch she was telling the truth. "I'm taking your name off our list of suspects," I told her.

"Oh, thank you," she gushed. You would have thought I'd just told her she'd won the lottery, she was so happy. "That is such a relief that you believe me."

"Phillip will, too," I told her.

"That's nice, but you're the one who matters to me." She looked at the pot in front of her, picked up a spoon, and tasted it. "That is terrible!"

"Hey, everybody has an off day," I said.

"Not me," she replied as she grabbed spice containers labeled CUMIN, OREGANO, and CAYENNE. After stirring some of each in, she tasted it again. "Better, but not perfect. I'll get it," she said. "Tell Trish it'll be ready in a minute and that we're going to have to replace the swill we've been serving with the good stuff."

"Tell her yourself," Trish said as she walked in. Clearly, she'd been eavesdropping on our conversation. "I'm glad you're back."

"I never left," Maggie said, and then quickly amended, "Well, not for very long, anyway."

Outside of the kitchen, Trish touched my shoulder lightly. "Thanks, Suzanne."

"I didn't do anything," I told her.

"I beg to differ. Go grab a chair with Phillip. The new and improved special will be right out. He already ordered for you both."

I took my seat, apologizing. "I tried to convince her that you should be there, but she..."

"Refused to talk in front of me," Phillip said. "Just tell me if you were able to get her to talk."

"She's got an alibi, and I already confirmed it," I said as I explained what had happened. "She could have set it up beforehand, but I don't think that's what happened."

"Her aunt sounds like a real charmer," Phillip said. "So Maggie's off the list for now. Suzanne, don't beat yourself up about me getting kicked out. It happens, and it might be you that's the one who is asked to leave next time."

"I just hope I can be as gracious about it as you are being right now," I said.

"Hey, Trish has been plying me with sweet tea, so it's all good. After we eat, I think we need to go have a word with Harrick Jackson."

The mere mention of the man's name spoiled my appetite, but only for a moment. I was looking forward to seeing how Maggie had managed to save the soup.

I knew one thing: it was going to be amazing.

Chapter 13

"AS MUCH AS I'D LIKE to hang around and have dessert, I think we should go talk to Harrick Jackson now," Phillip said after we finished our meal.

"I'm certainly curious to hear his explanation about that letter," I replied as we stood and headed to the cash register.

As Phillip tried to pay the bill, Trish said, "This one's on the house, folks. You got my cook back on track, and that makes us even as far as I'm concerned."

"All I did was listen, Trish. It's not that big a deal," I told her.

She leaned forward and said softly, "Suzanne, let me do this."

"Okay. Thanks," I said.

"Thank you," Phillip added as he started to put his money away. At least that was what it looked like to me, but then I saw that he'd palmed the ten that had been in his hand. As he tried to put the entire thing in the tip jar, Trish's hand lashed out and caught him.

"No, sir, that's not going to happen. Good try though."

Phillip grinned and put the money away for real. "Hey, you can't blame a guy for trying."

"Oh, I can and I do," Trish said with a grin, "but not this time. See you both later."

"Thanks again," I said.

"Thank *you*," she answered.

"I'm not talking to you two anymore," Harrick said when he came to his door. "I thought I made myself clear."

"We just figured you might like to discuss this with us before we turn it over to the police," Phillip said as he showed the copy of the handwritten note to Harrick.

"Don't try to deny that you wrote it," I said. "We had an expert analyze it, and he said that it was your handwriting." Our "expert" had been Phillip himself, but I wasn't about to point that out to our suspect. After all, in his own way, Phillip *was* an expert.

"Yeah? So what? That's ancient history," he said, trying to dismiss the note.

"I don't think so," I said. I read the message back to him.

"'You've lost your mind if you think I'm going to let you blackmail me. I'm warning you, if you try to use what you've got on me, I'll ruin you! Don't try to pet a snake; it will bite you every time.' There's so much in three little lines. You've admitted she was trying to blackmail you, and then you threatened her." I shook my head. "I'd say that showed motive enough for murder, wouldn't you, Phillip?"

"I would," he said. "Care to explain yourself? Last chance."

Instead of answering our questions, he asked one of his own. "Where did you get that, anyway? I wrote it sixteen years ago. Surely you didn't sit on it as evidence back then."

"No, it just came to light during our new investigation," Phillip said.

"So Arnie found it," Harrick surmised.

"We're not saying how we got ahold of it," I told him. "It looks bad for you, Harrick."

I could see that he thought about slamming the door in our faces. It was clear enough in his expression, but something must have changed his mind. Maybe he knew if he stonewalled us, we'd go straight to the police, which was what we were going to do anyway, but Phillip and I had wanted the first crack at him.

"It was nothing," Harrick said. "Just a misunderstanding."

"'I'll ruin you'? That doesn't sound like nothing to me," Phillip said.

"Okay, in the heat of the moment, I got upset with her. Susie Mae had been asking me for money for weeks, but I kept turning her down. She happened to overhear a conversation that wasn't meant for her ears, and she tried to use it against me. I was upset, so I wrote some things I regretted, but what you don't know is I found her an hour after she got that note, and we worked things out. We were good when she died."

"That's pretty convenient for you," I told him.

"Hey, it happens to be the truth," he protested.

"So what was she trying to blackmail you about?" Phillip asked.

"I was trying to put a deal together in Union Square to make some money, but I needed a piece of otherwise worthless land to make it happen. I lowballed the guy something awful, and he told me he'd need to think about it. I gave him twenty-four hours, and then I called my contact and told him we had our fish on the hook. We started talking about how much we were set to make on the deal when I heard something behind me. When I turned around, I saw Susie Mae standing there, smiling. She'd overheard everything, and after I hung up, she said that if I didn't pay her to keep quiet, she was going to go to the owner of the land and tell him what she'd overheard."

"Why put it in a note though?" I asked. "You could have just told her that to her face right then and there."

"I suppose I could have, but I didn't. As crazy as it sounds, it was the way Susie Mae liked to do things. She was a fool for letters and notes. Besides, I had to think about all of the angles before I confronted her, and she gave me an hour before she acted. She also said she didn't trust me face to face and that I could write it down or forget about it and she was going to talk. I didn't have much choice, and besides, I wanted her to worry about it a little. It's one thing to hear a threat, but it's another thing entirely to read it over and over again. I thought it would work on her, and in the end, it did. Like I said, as soon as she read the note, she came over to my place, and we worked it all out."

"How much did you pay her?" I asked, having a sudden insight into the situation. "You already admitted to loaning her money."

"That was before this even happened," he denied. "I didn't pay her a penny of blackmail money."

"But you said you worked it out," I pushed.

"I should have said it worked itself out. The guy called me before Susie Mae came over so we could talk about it and pulled out of the deal."

"Did he say why?" I asked.

"No, just that he was going to hold onto the property awhile longer, and there was nothing we could do to change his mind," Harrick said. "Deals are like that sometimes. You just need to win a few to come out ahead."

"You think Susie Mae went to him the second she read your note, don't you?" I asked.

He flinched for an instant, and I suspected that I had him. "No. She was bluffing, and we both knew it."

"So you say," Phillip answered.

"Hey, believe me or not, but like I said, we made up. We were good when she died, and I had nothing to do with it," he continued to protest.

"Did anyone else happen to know about your reconciliation?" I asked him.

"No, we kept it private, just between the two of us. There was no need to involve anyone else."

"So, we have just your word that things were good between you and a note that says it's possible that's not true at all," I told him. "You're also sticking to the story that you loaned her money before that, but you weren't concerned about her paying you back anytime soon. Is that all about right?"

Harrick stepped forward and got in my face before Phillip put an arm out and pushed him back. The man took a deep breath before he said anything else. "I told you what happened, and I don't appreciate being called a liar. Now leave me alone. Both of you."

As Harrick closed the door, I couldn't resist getting the last word in. "Or what, you'll bite us too?"

Harrick Jackson wanted to say something, I could see it in his eyes, but instead, he closed the door forcefully and left us on the front porch, alone.

"What do you think about that?" I asked Phillip as we walked back to my Jeep.

"I think you're better at poking bears than I am," he said with a wry grin. "Wow, I thought for a second there, he was coming after you."

"I did too, truth be told," I said. "I think I hit a nerve. What can we do about it now though? I think what I said was true. He loaned her some money, but then she came demanding more, this time as blackmail. They fought about it, but whether or not they made up or he killed her to shut her up, I couldn't say."

"Either way, we need to give the original note to Chief Grant," Phillip said. "He might be able to get fingerprints off it."

"We know Harrick's will be on it, and Arnie's too," I said.

"That's not the set I'm wondering about."

"You want to make sure Susie Mae's prints are on it too, don't you? Harrick already admitted to writing it."

"I know, but I just want to be sure," Philip answered.

"Fine, as long as I get to keep the copy we made," I replied.

"Absolutely," he said.

"After we drop the original off, what should we do?"

"I'd like to talk to someone else," he answered.

"I thought we'd already interviewed everyone involved."

"We have, but I'd still like to find out a little about Teddy Marcus."

"But he's dead," I protested. "It's going to be tough interviewing him without holding a séance."

"True, but his sister still lives in town. Maybe she knows something."

"I'd forgotten all about her. I suppose it's worth a try," I admitted.

We found Marla Simpson working at the grocery store, stocking shelves. She was a weathered woman, haggard enough to look a decade older than the forty years she had to her credit. "Hey, Marla," I said. "Do you have a second?"

"I'm just about to go on break, Suzanne," she said. "If you need something, ask Jerry."

"This is about your brother," Phillip said.

Her face went ashen. "Teddy's been gone a long time," she said softly. "There's nothing I can tell you about him."

"We were curious about his real relationship with Susie Mae," I told her.

"I don't want to talk about that. Like I said, I'm going on break now." She headed for the back door, but if she thought she was going to ditch us that easily, she was mistaken.

"You can talk to us now, or we can wait until you go back on duty," Phillip told her.

"Listen, I need this job. Since my husband left me, I'm taking care of two kids, and he hasn't paid a penny in child support."

I didn't want to throw her life into turmoil just for the sake of our curiosity, and I was about to back off when Phillip said, "Then you should talk to us. It will take three minutes of your time, and then you'll be done with us."

Marla shrugged. "Fine, but I'm smoking while we talk, so if you have a problem with that, you're just out of luck."

"That's fine," Phillip said.

Once we were back at the loading dock, Marla lit up, took a puff, and then waved it in our direction. "What do you want to know about Teddy?"

"What was his relationship with Susie Mae?" Phillip asked.

"They were friends," she said before taking another drag from her cigarette.

"We heard they were more than that," I told her. "Did you know your brother was sleeping with her behind Arnie Lancaster's back?"

Marla shrugged. "He was a grown man. He could do whatever he wanted to, even if it was a mistake."

"So then you knew about it at the time," Phillip said.

"Sure, I knew. The fooling around didn't bother me as much as the money she weaseled out of him. I told him the only reason she slept with him was to get what little cash he had, but he wouldn't believe me, and by the time he found out I was right, it was too late."

"We keep hearing that Susie Mae wanted money," I told her. "Do you know why?"

"She told Teddy she had an investment opportunity that was going to set her up for life," Marla said. "She claimed he'd get his money back and then some, but she got herself killed, and Teddy was in the hole until the day he died. I wish he'd never met her. The doctors say cancer killed him, but I think it was the poison of knowing Susie Mae Long."

Wow, those were strong words. "Did he hate her enough to kill her?" Phillip asked her.

"Hate her? He told me he was in love with her, even after she screwed him over! She could do no wrong in his eyes. He would rather have killed himself than hurt one hair on her head, and that's the truth." She finished her cigarette and lit another. At the rate Marla was smoking, she might be joining her brother sooner than she wanted to.

"But you didn't care for her, did you?" I asked her. "Is it possible you hated seeing her taking advantage of your brother, and you got rid of her yourself?"

"It's possible," she admitted. "That's why I'm glad I had an alibi."

"What is it, if you don't mind us asking?" Phillip asked.

"I don't have much say in the matter anyway, do I? Look it up. I got arrested for shoplifting in Maple Hollow that afternoon, and my folks decided to teach me a lesson and let me sit in a jail cell all night to show me the error of my ways. Guess what? It didn't work."

"What's that got to do with Teddy?" Phillip asked again. "He still could have done it."

"I *know* he didn't. He was working on getting me out the entire time. When my folks wouldn't bail me out, he stepped up. The irony is that if he hadn't given all of his cash to Susie Mae, he could have afforded to get me out in a second, but as it was, he had to drive to Asheville to get the money from our cousin. No, Teddy didn't kill Susie Mae, no matter what you might think of him. He was so torn up about her dying that he just about killed himself then and there. The money never really mattered to him. He loved her, and when she died, he went into a tailspin that he never could pull himself out of." She stubbed the cigarette out on the dock and said, "My break's over. Honest, I got nothing else for you. Don't come back in, okay?"

"Okay. We'll leave you alone," I told her. "Thanks for your time."

We'd clearly tortured the woman enough.

"So we can strike Teddy's name off our list," Phillip told me. "I remember hearing about Marla getting arrested, and Teddy is the one who put up her bail five hours after she was booked. I never knew why it took him so long, but it makes sense."

"I feel bad for Marla," I said suddenly.

"Suzanne, we make choices in this life, some good and some bad, but they all end up leading us to where we are right now," Phillip said.

"That's kind of a cynical point of view, isn't it?"

"Try being a cop and then tell me I'm being cynical," Phillip said. "Once you've lived that life, it's hard to ever be wide-eyed and innocent again."

"I'm not like that," I protested, though in truth I was, at least a little. "I'm not some innocent."

"I didn't say you were," he answered quickly, trying to mollify me. "Now, are you ready to go talk to Lucy again? It should go a lot easier this time."

"I sure hope so, because it couldn't go much worse," I agreed.

During the drive to Union Square we chatted some, but mostly, we kept our thoughts to ourselves. We'd learned a lot so far, and we'd even managed to eliminate a few suspects along the way, but the ones I cared about most were still on our list, and I hated it.

We needed to find out what really happened sixteen years earlier so we could put this murder behind us once and for all.

Chapter 14

"IS IT SAFE TO COME in?" Phillip asked Lucy as he poked his head in the door at Crafty Corner.

"Of course it is," she told him. "Didn't Suzanne tell you that I'm sorry for the way I acted yesterday? I know you two are only trying to help. I shouldn't have reacted the way I did."

"It's understandable," Phillip answered. "Have you had a chance to think about what might have happened to Susie Mae?"

"I have," she said and called out to an older woman with a blue vest on that signified a Crafty Corner employee. "Marjorie, I'll be in back if you need me."

"Yes, ma'am," she said as she took over Lucy's spot at the cash register.

"Let's go back to my office," Lucy said.

We followed her through the store, past aisles of yarn, card stock, fake flowers, artists' canvases, paints, and a thousand other items. Keeping track of everything had to be a nightmare, and I was glad yet again that I was in the donutmaking business. Lucy led us into a small space carved out of the cramped back storage area, but at least there were three chairs there.

"Sorry for the mess," she said as she moved a few order books off the chairs. "Cleaning up this office seems to be my last priority. I'm behind on a dozen things."

"We won't take up much of your time," I said. "Maybe you can shed some light on something for us. Susie Mae was going around getting money from just about every man she met. Do you happen to know why?"

"Actually, it was my fault," Lucy replied, catching me off guard completely.

"*Your* fault? Why did you need money?" Phillip asked her.

"To open this shop," she said as she swung her arms around the place. "Susie Mae and I were going to be partners, but we didn't have enough cash to get started. I had worked in a few craft shops in Atlanta, and I'd saved some money but not nearly enough. Susie Mae wanted to go into business with me, but I told her she needed a stake too, and she didn't have much money at all."

"That explains why she was getting loans from all of her friends," I said.

"I still feel terrible about it," Lucy said. "Not a day goes by that I don't feel responsible for what happened to her, even though I never saw a dime of the money she'd collected. I had to scrape by after she died and find a way to make it happen on my own, but I still feel guilty about making her chip in."

"Why do you say that?" I asked her.

"Isn't it obvious? If she hadn't needed money to buy into the venture, she wouldn't have crossed the wrong man."

"Do you still think a man killed her?" Phillip asked her.

Lucy seemed surprised by the question. "Don't you?"

"I asked you first," my stepfather said with a shrug.

"I just always naturally assumed that it was a man," Lucy answered as she settled back into her chair. "After all, Susie Mae always gravitated to men, and the attraction was mutual. She didn't have many women friends at all."

"How about Gabby Williams?" I asked.

"I don't think you could call them friends," Lucy said. "More like rivals. They had the same taste in men, and whenever a guy had a choice between Susie Mae and Gabby, they almost always chose my sister."

"That would give her reason enough not to like your sister," I said.

"Sure, but she wouldn't kill her," Lucy said.

"You seem certain of that," Phillip said.

"Gabby might have gone after Susie Mae with that bitterly sharp tongue of hers, but she wouldn't kill her. Not Gabby, certainly not by strangling her. That sounds like a man in a fit of rage to me."

"It was from behind though," I pointed out. "Doesn't a fit of anger mean it should have been from the front?"

"Not everyone could look someone in the eye while they choked the life out of them," Lucy said, her voice breaking a little as she said it. Discussing this had to be hard on her, but she'd invited us this time, not the other way around.

"Whoever did it could have grabbed that scarf from behind to catch Susie Mae off guard," Phillip said. "That's what I thought at the time. She wouldn't have had much chance to resist if she didn't know it was coming."

"Could we *please* discuss another aspect of the case? I can't bear the thought of my sister having the life squeezed out of her," Lucy said.

"You keep mentioning the men in her life," I said. "Do you have any other suspects in mind now that you've had time to think about it?"

"Do you mean besides Arnie and that list I gave you this morning?" she asked.

"I do," I said. "Unless you have new and direct evidence against Arnie Lancaster, just know that we haven't ruled him out, but we're keeping our options open at this point. I noticed this morning that Teddy Marcus wasn't on your list." I was trying to confirm Marla's story from another independent source if I could.

"I *know* it wasn't him," she said.

"How do you know that?" Phillip asked.

"He was bailing that no-good sister of his out of jail when it happened," she said. "He told me all about it at the funeral, how if he'd only stayed in town, he might have been able to save Susie Mae's life, like he was some kind of protector. If his name's on your list, I'd strike it off."

"That confirms what we've already heard," I told her. It was good to get someone to back up Marla's alibi for her brother, even if it wasn't new information.

"I always just assumed it was Arnie, but if it wasn't, it *had* to be Harrick or Parker," she said confidently.

"But not George Morris," Phillip offered.

I wasn't going to mention the mayor's name until someone else brought it up, and it surprised me that Phillip had.

"No, not George. I know I put him on my list this morning, but I was wrong to do that. Sure, he had a crush on my sister, but most men around here did. She was a real looker. That picture they ran in the paper today didn't do her justice."

"What did you think about the article?" I asked.

"Everybody knows Ray Blake isn't all that much of a stickler when the truth is involved. He does what he does to sell newspapers. I don't think he cares one whit about justice for my sister like you two do."

"So you weren't upset by what you read?" Phillip asked me.

"Of course I was upset," Lucy snapped, showing a bit of the anger we'd seen the day before. "He basically came out and called my sister a tramp! She can't defend herself from the grave, and I know better than to go after him myself. He could shut this place down if I gave him enough reason to turn his sights on me. No, I'm going to do my best to ignore it. Ray will lose interest soon enough."

"That's big of you," I said.

"Big nothing. He's got a heavy stick around here, and he's not afraid to use it. If I thought confronting him would do any good, I'd be in his office right now instead of here with you, but it would only hurt me, so what does it matter? Susie Mae's been gone sixteen years. I care about what people think about her, but I've got a business to protect. After all, it's all I've got. Our folks are gone, Susie Mae's gone, and I never got around to getting married and having a family of my own. It's so sad I try not to think about it most days, but what are you going to do?"

I felt bad for her, but there was really nothing I could say to that. "Did you know she threatened to expose Harrick Jackson in a shady deal he was trying to make? She tried to blackmail him."

"I don't believe that!" Lucy said. "I know I pressured Susie Mae for money, but she wouldn't go that far."

Phillip brought the copy of the letter Arnie had found out of his pocket and handed it to her. As she read it, her face got hot, and she was clearly angry by the time she finished reading the brief note. "What more proof do you need? Isn't it clear he killed her?"

"We're looking into it," Phillip reassured her, "but you said you thought Parker might have done it as well."

"The truth is that I never trusted Parker Henson," Lucy said. "He was always watching us from next door whenever we left the house, spying on us with binoculars when we sunned in the back yard. The guy has been a creep his entire life."

"Did you see anything that we might be able to use the next time we interview him?" Phillip asked.

"Ask him about Susie Mae's bedroom window," Lucy said with a frown.

"What about it?" I asked.

"It faced the Henson house, and we caught him peeping on her one night. He denied it, but it was obvious it was true. My folks spoke to his parents, but nothing came of it, and Mom and Dad moved Susie Mae to the den and put in heavy drapes so Parker couldn't spy on us anymore."

"He said you were the one who told him about Susie Mae," I said. "Was that true?"

"Yes. No. Probably. I was out of my mind with grief, so I could have gone over there to tell his folks what happened. I don't remember if he was there or not."

"You dated him even after he spied on you and your sister?" I asked her.

"That was years later. I knew I shouldn't have, but he was a smooth talker, and I was lonely. Parker took advantage of that, and it turned out that it was all just to get close to my sister. We went out a few times, but it was pretty clear from the start that he was fixated on Susie Mae. I didn't let it worry me. Back then, I was pretty enough on my own to attract my share of boys, believe it or not. But Parker was bad news then, and he's bad news now. If Harrick didn't kill Susie Mae, then surely it was him."

"Okay, we'll push him a little harder too," I promised.

"Don't give up on Arnie yet though," she insisted, and then she turned to my stepfather. "Phillip, I said it yesterday, and I'll say it again. I still believe with all my heart that you got the real killer back then. Don't let Arnie convince you otherwise. He's got a way of getting what he wants, and he always has. How else do you think he got Susie Mae to go out with him in the first place?"

"Like I said, we're looking at all three of them," I said. "Is there anything else you can think of?"

"No, that's it, but do me a favor. As soon as you figure out who killed Susie Mae, come find me, would you? I haven't slept a good night's sleep since she died sixteen years ago. Knowing who did it, who really did it, may be the only peace I ever get."

"We'll let you know," I assured her.

Once we were outside, Phillip said, "We need to go back to April Springs and ask Parker about his obsession with Susie Mae."

"Do you think he killed her?" I asked as I started driving.

"I've seen that kind of thing happen before," Phillip explained. "When a certain type of person can't get what they want so desperately, they do their best to make sure that no one else can get it either."

"It sounds like a crazy motive for murder to me," I said.

"'Crazy' is the operative word," Phillip agreed. "But Parker could be our man."

"Do you think Lucy's right?"

"About what in particular?" my stepfather asked.

"That a man must have done it," I explained.

"I'm not willing to say that yet, but it seems likely to me, too."

"Because our only female suspect left is Gabby Williams?" I asked.

"I know Gabby can be acerbic at times, but I don't see her killing Susie Mae over their rivalry, can you?" he asked me.

"I don't even like her name being on our list, but she lied to us about her alibi, and that needs to be addressed, whether we like it or not."

"Tell you what. Let's swing by ReNEWed before we tackle Parker again so we can clear this mess up with Gabby. What do you say?"

"I say that's a great idea. How about George?"

"He has to stay for now, regardless of what Lucy just said, but I'd be shocked if he turned out to be the killer, and it's not easy to surprise me anymore."

"I'd be more than shocked," I admitted. "I wouldn't believe it. There's no way he could kill someone, especially like that."

Phillip shrugged. "I'm not disagreeing with you. All I'm saying is that his name needs to stay right where it is."

"You can keep George and Gabby's names on your list if you want to, but mine is down to three," I told him.

"Parker, Harrick, and Arnie, just like Lucy's?" he asked.

"What do you know? You got it on the first guess," I confirmed.

"I tend to agree with you, but we can't ignore everyone else. We have to know."

"That's why we're doing this," I reminded him. "Sometimes not knowing is far worse than learning a truth that hurts, especially when it comes to murder."

"Or even life," Phillip mused as we made our way back to April Springs.

Chapter 15

"GABBY, WE NEED TO TALK," I said as Phillip and I walked into ReNEWed together the moment we got back to April Springs. At least her few customers were at the far end of the store, so if we kept our voices at a reasonable level, they wouldn't know we were interviewing Gabby about a murder.

"I have customers," she said, waving her hand in that general direction.

"This is important," I insisted.

"Why did you lie to us, Gabby?" Phillip asked her abruptly.

I'd been planning on being a bit more subtle than that, but maybe my stepfather was right. Gabby never danced around issues, so why should we?

"What are you talking about, Phillip?"

"We know you weren't with Teddy Marcus when the murder happened," I said softly. "Gabby, we need the truth."

She looked at me and then Phillip before she walked away.

That hadn't gone well.

But then she approached her customers. "Sorry, but we're closed."

One of the women protested. "But you're supposed to be open for hours more yet. We drove here all the way from Hickory."

"It's just for thirty minutes," Gabby told them, and then, to mollify them, she added, "When you come back, I'll give you five percent off your purchases to make up for the inconvenience."

"Make it ten and you've got a deal," the woman said shrewdly.

"Seven, and that's my final offer," Gabby answered with a frown.

"We'll see you in half an hour," she said as she grabbed her friend's arm. "Come on, Trudy. Let's get out of here."

"I'm sorry you had to give them a discount," I said, knowing full well how much Gabby hated giving anyone a break on her prices.

"I was willing to give her twenty percent, so it's a victory in my book," Gabby answered after she'd locked the door behind the women. "Now, how did you find out I was lying?"

"We spoke with Marla," I said.

"I was afraid of that. Suzanne, you're too good at this." Almost as an afterthought, she added, "You too, Phillip, but I expect it of you. After all, you were a cop, but this one," she said, pointing to me, "has continued to show she's better suited for your old job than you were."

For Gabby, that was high praise indeed, but I wasn't there to have my ego stroked. "Gabby, where were you really?"

"Were you with Harrick Jackson?" Phillip asked, voicing the hunch he'd had earlier.

She looked miserable for a moment then took a deep breath and said, "Yes. There, are you happy?"

"Why keep it a secret?" I asked her.

"Do you think I'm *proud* of being with him?" Gabby asked. "Why do you think I hid it for all these years?"

"I find it hard to believe you would risk arrest just to protect your reputation," Phillip said.

"What risk? You never suspected me until you and Suzanne started digging into Susie Mae's murder. I wasn't in any danger of prosecution, and I figured if I could save a little face, what did a little white lie hurt anybody?"

"You're going to need to do better than that," I told my friend. In a way, I wasn't surprised at all that she'd lied. Gabby wasn't above shading the truth in her favor on occasion, but I thought we were closer than that. Maybe if it had been Grace and me investigating instead of Phillip, she would have come clean from the start. I didn't know, but it still shook me a bit.

"You're right, I do." Before she got into her explanation, she took my hands in hers. "Suzanne, I'm sorry I lied to you." It was clear this apology was just for me. "Arnie showing up again caught me off guard, and I panicked. Forgive me."

I had never heard my friend speak so sincerely.

If she was telling the truth this time.

But I couldn't go around thinking the people closest to me were lying to my face. That might even be true on occasion, but it was certainly no way to live. I'd trust the people I loved, and if that ended up biting me later, then so be it. "It's okay, but why?"

"I was ashamed, plain and simple," Gabby answered contritely. "I thought I was getting one over on Susie Mae. I knew she'd been seeing Harrick on the side, and I wanted to pay her back for stealing Arnie from me. I know it was foolish and petty, but I let my vanity get the better of me. I had no idea Harrick was using me, not the other way around. When I found out the day after the murder, he confessed that he'd been using *me* to make Susie Mae jealous. He was going to tell her the next day about our little fling and tell her that she had to choose, or he would do it for her. I was just a pawn in his sick little game, and it embarrassed me so much I wanted to crawl into a hole and die. What did a little white lie hurt? Teddy is long dead."

"Still, sixteen years is a long time to hold that kind of grudge," Phillip said.

"Let me ask you something. Who dumped you at senior prom to go with your best friend?" Gabby asked him.

"Betsy Grayson," he answered quickly.

"That was a lot more than sixteen years ago," she pointed out. "How many people in your life know it happened?"

"Now that you've told Suzanne, just two, besides Betsy and Chuck," Phillip admitted.

"There you go," she said.

"Okay, I get what you're saying, but you could have given Harrick an alibi, and he could have told us himself and saved himself a great deal of grief," I answered.

"Trust me, he won't say a word unless it's under oath," Gabby said smugly.

"Why is that?" Phillip asked.

"Let's just say that ten years ago, some information about something entirely unrelated to Susie Mae came to my attention about Harrick Jackson, and his silence about him playing me for a fool was one of the conditions of me keeping my mouth shut," Gabby replied, clearly satisfied that she'd finally gotten the upper hand on the man. It wouldn't even have surprised me to learn that Gabby had sought out that hold herself.

"Is it illegal, what he did?" the former chief of police asked.

"What it is is none of your business. All you need to know is that I'm telling you the truth now."

"You know, you could have helped Harrick by telling us from the start," I said.

"You're right. I could have," she said with a broad grin. "But what fun would that have been?"

"Wow, whatever hold you have over him must be pretty strong," I told her.

She just shrugged. "I'm truly sorry about lying to both of you," she said, nodding toward Phillip as well this time.

"We understand," I told her, and Phillip even nodded. I promised myself to try to forget all about Betsy Grayson and what she'd done to my stepfather on prom night. Some things were better left buried in the past, where they belonged.

But not murder.

There was a reason there wasn't a statute of limitations on homicide.

We owed the victims at least that much.

"Well, at least we've confirmed that theory," I said once we were standing on the sidewalk in front of ReNEWed and the shoppers were readmitted.

"I suspected as much, but I didn't want it to be true. It's really a shame, because I was starting to like Harrick Jackson for the murder."

"Do we need to ask him about Gabby's story to see if it's true?" I asked. I hated the thought of pursuing it any further, but I always tried to verify alibis whenever I could during the course of my investigations.

"Why bother? He'd just lie to us again," Phillip said. "I'd love to know what Gabby has on him, but I believe her."

"So do I," I told him. "That limits our list of suspects to two."

"Parker Hanson and Arnie himself," Phillip admitted.

"Let's go see Parker then," I answered.

"You know, Arnie still could have done it," Phillip said as we got into my Jeep and drove to the man's house.

"I know," I answered. "What I don't get is why he'd ask us to prove his innocence if he knew all along that he was the killer."

"Hubris, plain and simple," Phillip replied. "He always did think he was smarter than me."

"Well, he would be wrong," I answered. "If he did it, we'll find a way to prove it."

"You'd better believe we will. I hate being played for a fool."

"You're not the only one," I said, thinking of not only Gabby but myself too. If Arnie had been playing with us, I was going to make it my life's ambition to wreck him. He might not be able to stand trial for the murder again, but he was going to pay, one way or the other. There wouldn't be anything malicious about it, either.

It would simply be a matter of small-town justice.

"Something's been bothering me about this, and I just realized what it was," Phillip admitted as I drove.

"Did you finally figure out what you couldn't put a finger on before?"

"I think so. From all we've heard, Susie Mae was collecting money from everyone. It's probably what got her killed, one way or the other."

"Agreed," I said.

"So where is it?" Phillip asked. "Lucy claims she never got a penny of it. I'm guessing it had to be well over twenty grand, and that's being conservative, but she didn't have more than a hundred dollars to her name when we checked her out. I didn't think anything of it at the time, because nobody but Arnie mentioned money back then, and I discounted that as him trying to divert our attention from the argument they'd had."

"Do you think the killer murdered her for the cash and took it from her after he killed her?" I asked.

"It's certainly possible," Phillip said.

"Did Arnie have any extra money when you arrested him?" I asked.

"No."

I had a sudden thought. "Could that be where he really was last night?"

Phillip got it instantly. "Are you thinking that he really wasn't going after Harrick at all, that he was retrieving the money he'd hidden after he killed Susie Mae?"

"It's a possibility," I said. "It's just a shame we can't get a search warrant and look through that house for the missing cash."

"We're not cops. If I've learned anything from you in the past, it's to act and ask for forgiveness later rather than permission."

"Why, Phillip Martin, I do believe you're coming around to my way of thinking," I said with a grin. "How do we do it though? We're the ones who told him not to leave the house. We can't very well get him to leave so we can search it, now, can we?"

"I have an idea if you're game," he said.

"You know me. I'm always game."

"Okay, here's what we should do."

As he explained his plan, I pulled the Jeep over so I could give him my full attention. It wasn't all that risky, and it might just garner us the information we were after.

At the very least, it was worth a shot, so I diverted our drive to Arnie's instead. There was no time like the present.

"What are you two doing here?" Arnie asked as he came to the door. "Did you find more evidence about Harrick?"

"We may have," Phillip said, "but we need your help."

"It's about time," Arnie answered. "What can I do?"

"I want to confront him with that letter," Phillip said, though we'd already done just that.

"What took you so long?"

"I thought it would be better if you did it with me," Phillip replied.

"Now you're talking. Between the three of us, we'll crack that nut. Just you watch," he said enthusiastically.

That wasn't part of our plan, but Phillip had foreseen it, and he had an answer for it. "He's not going to talk in front of her," my stepfather said as he gestured toward me. "We may need to muscle him a bit to get him to admit anything." That was pure fabrication, but I tried my best to look timid, not a disposition I had ever tried to portray before.

"That's true enough. Sometimes a little brute force is what it takes. What are you going to do while we talk to Harrick?" he asked me.

"I'd go home, but I'm a little afraid of being there alone, what with a killer on the loose and all," I said, the words nearly sticking in my throat even as I said them. Playing a damsel in distress was definitely not in my wheelhouse, but it was necessary, so I bit the bullet and did it.

"Could she stay here, Arnie? Nobody would look for her here, in case Harrick is out there trying to hunt her down."

"Why would he do that?" Arnie asked as he kept glancing at me.

"He's probably afraid I know something," I replied meekly.

"Yeah, I can see that. Sure, you can hang around here. Just don't mess with my stuff, okay? I know it looks like a mess, but I've got it organized so I can deal with it later."

"I won't touch one single thing," I said, which was the literal truth. I planned on touching dozens and dozens of them in my search while they were gone, not just one.

He wasn't too happy about it, that much was obvious, but Phillip slapped his old friend on the back and said, "Let's go before he figures out that we're on his trail and runs!"

"Okay, I'm with you," he said.

"Suzanne, I need the keys to your Jeep," Phillip said.

I didn't let anyone but Jake drive it, but it was part of the plan, so I handed them over. "Take good care of her, Phillip."

"She won't get a scratch on her on my watch," he said, and then they were gone.

I figured I'd have half an hour before Phillip would find a reason to stop hunting for Harrick and come back. We'd decided there was no way the two men could confront Harrick with something he already knew about without blowing our whole story, so we'd devised a ruse that would lead them on a wild goose chase across town, everywhere but Harrick's house, where we were pretty sure he was.

It was time to get busy.

Chapter 16

AS I SEARCHED, I MOSTLY found junk, the flotsam and jetsam people collect in their lives. The main areas got a perfunctory look, since I didn't have a great deal of time. I was counting on Phillip being able to keep Arnie occupied, but that was not guaranteed. I could mostly tell what had belonged to Arnie's late father, so I concentrated on the guest bedroom, where a few boxes marked ARNIE were stored. As he'd promised, things were more organized in there. I was kind of surprised that he hadn't moved into the main bedroom, but then again, with images of the ghost of his late father there, it made more sense that he'd go back to his childhood bedroom.

None of the boxes yielded anything interesting, let alone the missing cash.

I took photos of everything before I touched it so I could put it all back exactly the way I'd found it. They had the added benefit of giving me something to refer to later after my search was over. I emptied the stacked boxes in the closet one at a time, moving them each carefully out into the hallway as I searched them.

I was about to put them back where I'd found them after I was through when I noticed that one edge of the old heart pine floorboard in the back was lifted a little higher than the rest. Getting down on my hands and knees, I tried to pry the loose board up, but I couldn't get a good enough grip on it. Finally, I went into the kitchen and retrieved a butter knife. Sliding it carefully between the loose board and the one beside it, I was finally able to get it to release.

I was hoping to find money, lots and lots of money, hidden there, but instead I found something that might have been even more interesting.

There was a small shoebox in the cavity, and when I lifted the lid, I found letters from Arnie's past girlfriends, including Susie Mae. As a matter of fact, the majority of the letters and notes to Arnie were from her. It seemed she truly had loved communicating that way, and evidently, she demanded them from the men in her life as well if the note from Harrick was any indication.

Most of them made me blush, and a few of the enclosed Polaroids were much too much for my taste, but the last letter I found from Susie Mae was the one that caught my attention.

Arnie,

It's over. There is nothing you can say to get me back, all right? Give up.

You'll get your money back, don't worry about that. I'm good for it. It just may take a while.

Stop following me, stop calling me, stop stalking me.

I mean it. We're through.

Susie Mae.

Wow. The fight they'd had must have been after Arnie wouldn't take "no" for an answer in the note. Instead of accepting the dismissal, he'd clearly confronted her about it, thus the argument that was later used against him in court. It confirmed what Phillip had believed from the beginning, that Arnie had every reason in the world to be furious with Susie Mae. I took a photo of the letter and put everything back in its place. As I was lowering the box, I saw something just beyond it under the floorboards, but I couldn't make out what it was.

I used the flashlight on my phone, and that cleared up considerably. It was a thousand dollars, cash.

But that was all that was there. If he had more, I had no idea where he'd stashed it or why this grand was flying solo.

That barely touched what Susie Mae had gotten from everyone, and it might not even have come from her stash, but it didn't look good for Arnie. I was just setting the floorboard back in place when I heard something creak behind me.

I wasn't alone!

Chapter 17

"WHAT ARE YOU DOING, Suzanne?" Arnie asked me angrily. "Why is all my stuff out in the hallway?"

I had to come up with something, and fast. "I was bored, so I thought I'd look around out front when a mouse darted out of one of those boxes and ran into this room. I was just moving these things to find him when I heard you. Help me look! They can do a lot of damage."

"Yeah, Pop wasn't the cleanest guy in the world," Arnie said as he set two of his boxes back on top of his hiding place. I saw him study the loose board, but evidently, he didn't find any evidence that I'd found his hoard of letters and cash.

"You really need to get some traps," I told him.

"Yeah, I'll do that."

I looked around. "Hey, where's Phillip?"

"Beats me," Arnie said, moving more things back until the closet was completely blocked again.

"You were supposed to stay together," I chided him.

"Well, he didn't have the slightest clue where Harrick was, so I ditched him." Arnie took a step toward me, and I felt a chill of uncertainty ripple through me.

"He's not going to like that you left him," I told him as I started maneuvering toward the door. Had Arnie done something to Phillip, and was I next on his list? I couldn't discount it, and I looked quickly around for something, anything I could use as a weapon to defend myself.

"I don't like you being in here," Arnie said, his good nature that I'd seen exhibited earlier now gone. "In the joint, you don't have any privacy, and that's one of the things I missed most."

"I'm sorry. I was just trying to help," I said as I kept scanning the space for a weapon.

There was nothing I could use though.

He was about to say something else when Phillip burst into the room. "There you are. Arnie, where did you go?" My stepfather looked relieved to see that I was okay, but he couldn't have been any happier than I was to see him.

"I'm not a patient man, Phillip. You should know that better than anyone else around here."

"We still have a few places to look for Harrick," my stepfather told him.

"You go do it, and take Suzanne with you. I've got some things I need to do here."

I was positive Arnie was going to check on his stash the moment we were gone to see if I'd touched it. I just hoped that I'd put everything back where it belonged. Otherwise, he would know that I'd found it, and his secrets.

"Come on, Suzanne. Let's go," Phillip said.

I had no trouble following that particular order. "We'll be back later, Arnie," I told him. "Will you be here?"

"I'm not chasing any more wild geese if that's what you're asking," he told me.

"Good enough."

Once we were outside and back in my Jeep, Phillip said, "I'm sorry, Suzanne. He slipped out when I stopped the car at a light. I tried to call and warn you, but I couldn't get an answer."

I pulled out my phone and saw that I must have accidentally switched it to silent mode again. It happened all the time, and I was getting sick of it. I was going to have to get myself a new phone when I got the chance, but in the meantime, I had to be more careful.

"Sorry about that."

"Did you find anything? I know you didn't have much time, so don't feel bad if you didn't."

"As a matter of fact, I got lucky. I was going through the boxes in his closet when I found a loose floorboard," I told him. Once I'd taken the keys and driven us down the block a ways, I pulled over and retrieved my phone. Sure enough, it had switched itself to silent again in my pocket. What a piece of junk. I loved technology in general, but it did come with its own problems and complications at times. "Check this out," I said as I showed him the letter from Susie Mae.

"So she broke up with him in a note, but he wouldn't let it go, so he confronted her in public, thinking she wouldn't have the nerve to dump him face to face."

"Boy, was she wrong," I said. "That's not all I found. Besides a pile of steamy letters and photos I tried my best to ignore, I found this." I flipped to the next picture, but all I could see was a flesh-colored blur.

"What's that, your finger?"

"Blast it, I was rushing, and I missed it. There was money there, too."

"Twenty grand?" he asked me.

"No, it was just a thousand, but that doesn't mean that it didn't come from Susie Mae's stash," I said.

"If we had a photo, we could check the dates of the numbers on the bills," Phillip said.

"Hey, I know I messed up, so there's no reason to rub it in," I answered a bit curtly.

"I wasn't blaming you for anything," he said quickly. "It's a miracle you found anything at all, given the little amount of time you had. That was some good police work there."

That made me feel a bit better. "I'm just sorry I missed the last shot. Should we go back to Arnie's and confront him with what I found?"

"No, let's let him simmer a bit," Phillip said. "We need more than we've got before we go after him again. Right now, I'd still like to pay Parker Henson another visit."

"Even after what I just found?" I asked.

"I jumped the gun once before on this case," the former chief of police said. "I promised myself it wouldn't happen again."

"You're right," I agreed. "Besides, Arnie isn't going anywhere. He thinks he's in the clear."

"Maybe he is, and maybe he's not, but for the moment, let's give him some space and head over to Parker's place."

"I don't want to talk to you," Parker said as he answered our knock.

"Don't be that way, Parker. We've got something you need to hear," Phillip answered calmly. "Now, are you going to invite us inside, or do we have to do it out here, where all of your neighbors can see?"

"I'm not letting you into my house," he said resolutely as he stepped out and closed the door behind him. "Say what you've got to say, and then go."

I looked over at the house where Susie Mae and Lucy had grown up, and then I glanced at Parker's place. "Let me guess. Your bedroom was right there," I said as I pointed.

He glanced in that direction. "Yeah. So what?"

"It was the perfect place to peep at Susie Mae," Phillip said. "What happened? Did you try something with her after she teased you, so you showed her once and for all who was boss? She had it coming, didn't she? Is that what you thought?"

Parker surprised me by lashing out and taking a swing at Phillip, but evidently, my stepfather had been expecting it. He sidestepped the punch, grabbed Parker's arm, and then twisted it behind his back.

"Let go of me!" Parker shouted, clearly not caring who heard him.

"Take it easy, son," Phillip said almost in his ear. "No need for violence."

"I said get your hands off me!" Parker jerked his arm hard, but all he managed to do was to tighten Phillip's grip.

"Why should I do that, so you can take another swing at me?"

"I'm calling the cops, the real cops, and having you arrested for assault!" The man was trying to be defiant, but I could see the tears forming in the corners of his eyes.

"You took the first swing at me, Parker," Phillip reminded him. "Who do you think the police are going to believe, a former chief or a Peeping Tom?" As he asked the question, he twisted Parker's arm a bit more.

I'd had enough. "Let him go, Phillip."

My stepfather looked at me in surprise, and then he must have caught something in my expression. He did as I asked, released Parker's arm, and then he took a step back. "Sorry."

"Your apology means nothing to me!" Parker spat out the words.

"I wasn't apologizing to you," Phillip said.

"Well, you should," Parker said, rubbing his shoulder. "Susie Mae *never* teased me. She made it clear I wasn't in her league, but I didn't care. If she'd had more time, she would have come around, I know it. But Arnie killed her before she could see what she had standing right in front of her." He was openly weeping now, but he didn't even seem to notice it. "I would never have hurt her," he said softly as he opened his door and slunk inside. I'd been expecting a slam, but it barely closed as he gently pulled it shut.

"What just happened there, Phillip?" I asked him as we headed back to my Jeep.

"I kind of lost it, didn't I? He got my adrenaline going when he took a swing at me. Thanks for talking me down."

"You're welcome. You surprised me," I told him flatly.

"Yeah, I surprised myself too," he answered. "Don't tell your mom, okay? I don't want her to think of me that way."

"Hey, you were protecting both of us," I told him, trying to make him feel better.

"We both know better than that, but thanks for saying it."

As we got into my Jeep, I asked him, "What now? Do we go back and talk to Arnie?"

"No, I think we need to let him stew tonight too. How sure are you that you put everything back in its proper place?"

"Well, he rushed me, but I think we're good," I replied.

"Then let's not do anything." He shook his head before he said, "I know it's way past suppertime, but if you don't mind, I think I'd like to head home, take a long, hot shower, and try to figure out how we should approach things tomorrow."

"It's okay, Phillip. You didn't do anything you need to worry about."

"I'm not sure I agree. If you hadn't been there, I might have done something much worse than I did."

I doubted that was true, but it had shown a side of my stepfather that he rarely exhibited. It must have come from all those years of being a cop. I'd seen Jake teeter on the brink of the same edge a few times in the past, mainly when someone was threatening me. It was hard sometimes to remember that these good-natured men in my life had another side to them, one that had developed after years of dealing with criminals of all kinds. I'd never faced that sort of adversity, and I hoped I never did.

"It'll all be fine after a good night's sleep," I told him as I drove him home.

"Do you have anything you can eat for dinner?" he asked me once I started to let him off at his place. "I should have at least fed you."

"Take care of yourself, and I'll worry about me," I told him with a slight laugh. "How about you?"

"I've got leftovers to last me a week," he happily admitted, "even though I'm not all that hungry at the moment."

"I'm sure I can scrape something up myself," I told him. "See you at eleven tomorrow morning, okay?"

"I'll be there," he promised.

I drove past the Boxcar Grill without stopping in. I felt like a peanut butter and jelly sandwich, which was about all I had in the house, so that worked out well for me. I needed a shower first though. I always felt better when I was clean, and tonight was no exception.

After my sandwich, I dug out the last of the bread pudding Momma had delivered earlier. I was shocked there was any left, since Jake was more addicted to the stuff than I was. Momma used day-old croissants from the grocery store for the bread base, and it was amazing.

On top of the container was a handwritten note from my dear, sweet husband.

"I love you more than bread pudding. Not by a lot, but just enough. Enjoy!"

It was the sweetest way to end the day I could think of. I heated it up and added a guilty-pleasure dollop of vanilla ice cream on top, took it into the living room, and put on a movie I'd seen a thousand times before. After I ate, I turned off the lights and watched until halfway through the flick, when I promptly fell asleep on the couch.

It wasn't until three hours later that I woke up.

Someone was on my front porch, and they must have stumbled in the dark and knocked over one of the new planters Jake and I had bought recently.

Apparently, I had an unexpected visitor.

I grabbed my softball bat from the hall closet and flipped on the light switch, hoping I could catch the intruder.

That turned out to be easier than I'd expected, because they were still sprawled out on the porch after their fall.

It was Parker Henson, and in his hand was something that didn't really surprise me at all.

It wasn't a gun but another Monopoly playing card.

Chapter 18

I DIALED 911 AS I PUSHED Parker back down with the end of my softball bat when he tried to get up. "This is Suzanne Hart. I caught my prowler. Tell the chief," I said.

"Hey, stop poking me! That hurts," Parker protested.

"Then stop trying to get up. Why did you kill her, Parker? Was Phillip right? Did you try to woo her and she rejected you?"

"What? No! I told you the truth before."

"Why don't I believe you?" I asked him as I had to poke him down again. This guy just wouldn't learn. "Why else would you want us to stop our investigation?"

"It's undignified!" he screeched. Wow, that was an odd word coming from a man sprawled on my front porch. "Besides, Arnie did it, but now he can't be punished for it. Let the poor girl rest in peace! It's the only decent thing to do!"

"You, sir, are a very bad liar. Let me tell you why you wanted to warn us off the investigation. We were getting close to you, too close, and you needed it to stop. What are we going to find when we dig into your life a little harder?" I had a sudden thought given Susie Mae's propensity to write and receive notes and letters. "If the police get a search warrant, are they going to find incriminating letters from the murder victim still in your possession?"

His face suddenly went white. "That doesn't prove anything!"

Chief Grant rolled up with his lights flashing and his siren blaring. Apparently, he'd taken my summons seriously.

After handcuffing Parker, the chief turned to me. "Thanks for calling."

"Hey, it was my pleasure. Phillip's on his way. He's still mad I called you first instead of him," I said. I'd phoned him right after I'd called the chief of police, and he hadn't been happy about being second.

"You can't arrest me! I didn't do anything," Parker started shouting as the chief put him in the back of his squad car.

"You threatened this woman, not once but twice," the chief said as Phillip drove up. "That's enough for now."

"Chief, I suspect he's held onto some incriminating evidence at his home," I said.

"Shut up, Suzanne! You're just a donutmaker," he cried out.

"A donutmaker that's going to see you go to jail," I told him.

"What's this evidence?" Chief Grant asked.

"Susie Mae seemed to be a chronic note and letter writer, and when I mentioned that to Parker, his face drained! I'm betting she threatened him, and the fool held onto it. What kind of hold did this woman have over these men? She was beautiful, but not enough to explain the mindless devotion these guys seemed to have for her."

"It wasn't just her looks," Phillip said as he joined us. "She was a true siren. The woman knew how to use every last ounce of her sex appeal. It was a weapon for her."

"A weapon that evidently backfired," Chief Grant said. "Chief Martin, would you like to come along with me for the interrogation?"

"I'd be honored," he said before glancing at me. "If it's okay with you, Suzanne."

I stifled a yawn. "I have no problem with that. I'm just glad this mess is finally over."

"That makes two of us," Phillip said. "Are you going to call Jake and tell him?"

"Let's wait until he confesses," I said.

Phillip glanced over at the raging man in the back of the squad car. "It might be a long night, but we'll get him." He then turned to Chief Grant. "I'll follow you over there."

"Sounds good to me," he said.

Once they were gone, I was too wired to go to sleep. I knew Parker Henson had a volatile temper. He'd shown it when he'd attacked

Phillip, and who was to say that he hadn't done the same thing to Susie Mae when she'd rejected him?

It was like Phillip said.

Her sex appeal had ended up being her downfall.

Or had it?

Chapter 19

I STARTED THINKING about everything I'd learned about Susie Mae Long and the people she had surrounded herself with, and there was one person I'd discounted as a suspect, basically because of everything I'd heard about the murder victim and her relationship with men.

She'd also had a close love/hate relationship with a woman in her life.

Her sister, Lucy.

As far as I could tell, Lucy had been the only one to truly gain from Susie Mae's death. She'd been the one to demand money from her sister, and who was to say she didn't collect it before she killed her, regardless of what she'd told us earlier? She'd been jealous of her sister's success with men for most of her life. How bitter it must have been when men used her to get to Susie Mae! Had that been Lucy's plan all along, to get her sister in debt to all of the men in her life and then get rid of her once she had what she wanted? Or had there been a plan at all? We'd seen firsthand how volatile Lucy's temper was! She'd thrown us out of her store, and the anger she'd expressed had been real enough. Had she been upset about us reopening the investigation not because it would bring back bad memories but because it might end up sending her to jail? The more I looked at the crime and the evidence, the more it pointed to an act of instant anger. We'd all just assumed that it had been spawned by her treatment of men, not the way her sister perceived Susie Mae's actions.

Was I being crazy, or were things suddenly becoming clear?

I had to talk to her again, and it couldn't wait until morning.

"Lucy, it's Suzanne Hart. Do you have a second?"

"What's up, Suzanne? Did you find Susie Mae's killer?" she asked.

"Maybe," I answered. "That's what I'd like to talk to you about. Is this a good time for you? I would really like to clear a few things up while things are still fresh."

"I guess so," she said. "What do you need to know?"

"Let's do it in person, if you don't mind," I said. I figured I'd swing by the police station and pick Phillip up before I confronted the woman who might just be a killer. He probably wouldn't be happy about being dragged out of Parker's interrogation, but I knew he'd come with me if I asked him to. After all, he had Momma and Jake to answer to if anything happened to me, and I wasn't in the mood to do anything as reckless as interview the woman alone.

"That's fine. You'll have to come by the store though. I'm doing inventory, and my car's been acting up on me, so I don't trust it to make it all the way to April Springs."

"No worries. I'm on my way."

"See you soon," she said.

I thought about calling Phillip and giving him a heads-up that I was on my way, but knowing him, he'd have the ringer off on his phone so he wouldn't be interrupted during the interview session. I grabbed my jacket and my keys and headed out the front door.

I made it three steps before Lucy stepped out of the shadows, holding a knitting needle toward my heart as though it was some kind of divining rod of death.

Chapter 20

"GET BACK INSIDE, YOU blasted meddler," Lucy snapped as she got closer to my heart with that thin, sharp needle.

"You're *here*?" I asked numbly as I flipped my phone's voice memo app on before she noticed what I was doing. It was a skill I'd practiced over the years, so I managed to do it even without looking at my phone. I hoped. Either that, or I had opened a game of Solitaire I would probably never get a chance to play. If I'd done it correctly, at least there'd be a record of what had happened to me.

"Yeah, I lied to you. So what?" Lucy asked with a bitter smile. "You know, don't you?"

"Know what? I just wanted to ask you a few questions, that's all. Why are you acting like this?" I hated playing stupid, but what choice did I have? I had to buy some time until I could figure out what my next move was.

"Suzanne, I watched the entire thing play out from over there." She pointed to the shadows of the park that bordered my property. "I was about to knock on your door to try to find out how much you knew when that idiot Parker showed up and made a scene! I thought I was in the clear, but just in case, I decided to hang around a bit, and lo and behold, you called me to question me after everyone else thought they'd captured the killer. At that point, I knew you knew, so stop acting stupid. It doesn't become you."

"Fine. I know you did it," I told her. If I was going to die, I was going to go out defiantly, not like some weak, simpering rag. "Your own sister? Why? Was it about the money or the men? You got it, didn't you?"

"Why are you so surprised when people lie to you? What were you expecting, the truth? Sure, my sister. Haven't you ever heard of Cain and Abel? Why not women? As to why, she flaunted that money in my face and bragged about how the men were putty in her hands, that she had powers I'd never even be able to dream of. She used to make fun of me when we were kids, and it just got worse and worse over the years. I don't know what happened. Something snapped. The fool turned her back on me, and I saw the ends of her scarf dangling down her back, so I grabbed them and started twisting. It was easier than I thought it would be. She shouldn't have made fun of me. Really, she got what was coming to her. I took the money, and I opened Crafty Corner. I told you I did it with my inheritance, and in a way, it was true. Why should *she* be a part of my new business? She might have put up half the money in the beginning, but I'm the one who made it a success!"

This woman had justified her actions over the years since her sister's death to the point of believing that she hadn't even been in the wrong when she'd murdered her.

"You don't have to hurt me," I said as I looked over at a nearby table lamp, just a step away. It was heavy, an Arts and Crafts replica, and if I could hit her with it, I might be able to save myself. "I can't prove anything. It's just your word against mine."

"Yes, but people listen to you, Suzanne. I'm afraid I have no choice."

At that moment, my friend the owl hooted three times just outside.

It wasn't much, but it was all the distraction I was going to get.

As Lucy's glance shifted to the door for a split second, I dove for the lamp.

She saw what I was doing, but she wasn't fast enough to stop me.

Unfortunately, the fact that the lamp was heavy was a two-edged sword.

I didn't have time to swing it very hard, and I missed her head completely.

But I hit the hand with the metal skewer of a knitting needle, and it clattered to the floor.

She wasn't about to let that stop her though. Lucy grabbed for the needle, her weapon of choice, while I ripped the cord from the lamp and used it on her neck. I had to leap onto her back to get a good purchase on it, but I was in control now.

In a way, it was fitting to strangle a strangler, but I didn't apply the killing pressure that it would take to end her life.

I didn't even do it hard enough to make her pass out.

What I did do was get her attention.

Suddenly, she lost all interest in that needle weapon of hers and used her hands to claw at her throat, trying to break me loose.

I put my knee in her back, let go of the cord, and used my hands to bounce her head hard into the floor.

They were direct hits, and she had no way to protect herself.

I might have broken her nose, but I didn't care.

I'd beaten her, and Lucy had lost her last chance to get rid of me, once and for all.

Chapter 21

"THAT WAS A NICE TOUCH, using the power cord to wrap her hands up," Chief Grant said as he surveyed the scene.

"I'm afraid I killed that lamp, and it was Jake's favorite," I said as I noticed that my hands were shaking. It was often like that. I was fine in an emergency, but once it was over, I tended to fall apart.

"Given the circumstances, I think he'll forgive you," the chief said. "I'll get your phone back to you as soon as we transfer the conversation you two had. That was quick thinking to record it."

"I at least wanted you to know what happened to me if I didn't make it," I admitted. "I'm just glad it worked." I'd played the conversation back for him after he'd taken Lucy away, and sure enough, it was all there, muffled but still recognizable, which was all I had hoped for.

"Do you want to call your husband before I take it?" the chief asked.

"I already did. The funny thing is that Jake was already on his way when I called. He'll be here in half an hour, probably less from the way he sounded."

To my surprise, I saw headlights roaring up the road, and I knew it was my husband. "Or even sooner," I said.

Jake stopped the truck in the yard and raced out to embrace me. "I'm so glad you're okay."

"I broke your lamp," I confessed from the safe haven of his chest.

He started laughing. "I'm okay with that, Suzanne. What did I tell you about going to look for trouble on your own?"

"Hey, trouble came looking for me this time," I told him, not willing to give up the safety and warmth.

"It has a way of doing that, doesn't it?" Jake asked.

Chief Grant coughed once, and then he said, "I need to get Lucy over to the jail. Are you two coming? I'll need a statement, Suzanne, the sooner the better, while it's all still fresh in your mind."

"I'm not about to forget what happened, but we'll be right there," I told him.

Jake asked me, "Are you sure you're up to it?"

"She never laid a needle on me," I told him, feeling giddy from surviving the attack.

"It could have been bad though," Jake said softly, not willing to let me go any more than I wanted to be released.

"It wasn't though. Everything's okay, Jake."

"It is now," he said.

It took us a while to get to the station, but it was time well spent in my husband's arms. I didn't need him for me to be complete, but I surely loved having him around.

As we walked across the park to the station, holding hands, I marveled at how one sister could hate another one so much that she killed her.

I guessed there were just some things I would never understand, and that was okay with me.

I had a family of friends and loved ones that I'd never turn my back on, and that was all that counted with me.

I was home, in every sense of the word, and I planned on staying there for a very long time.

RECIPES

Cherry Mini-Fritters

It's no secret that I love fritters, and though apple is usually my go-to flavor, sometimes, I like to shake it up with cherry. When they cool just a bit, I dust them with powdered sugar and enjoy, though they can also be iced with a simple vanilla glaze. Whichever way you have them, remember, these treats were never meant to be low calorie, and this recipe is no exception, but like Suzanne says, we all need a treat every now and then!

Ingredients

3⁄4 cup all-purpose flour (I like unbleached all-purpose, but if all you have on hand is bread flour, it will work too)

1⁄4 cup white granulated sugar

1 tablespoon baking powder

1 tablespoon cinnamon

1⁄4 teaspoon salt

1⁄3 cup milk (whole, 2%, or 1%)

1 egg, beaten

1⁄2 cup fresh or frozen cherries, thawed, plus enough granulated white sugar to coat them

Enough oil to fry in, peanut or canola

Directions

Heat enough peanut or canola oil to 360°F while you mix the batter.

In a large bowl, sift the dry ingredients together, then stir in the milk and the beaten egg.

Fold in the cherry pie filling until everything is well incorporated, and then take a teaspoon of batter and rake it into the fryer with another spoon.

If the dough doesn't rise soon, gently nudge it with a chopstick, being careful not to splatter oil.

After 2 minutes, check your fritters, and then flip them, frying for another minute on the other side. These times may vary given too many factors to count, so keep a close eye on them so they don't overcook.

Makes about a dozen mini-fritters.

Cinnamon Nutmeg Donut Treats

Here's a variation on one of my new air fryer recipes. They aren't quite ready for prime time yet, but I'm making headway in producing light and airy donuts with just some of the calories of the fried ones.

As I've said before, try this one with a measure of forgiveness in your heart if they don't turn out well for you. If you want to wait until I'm a little more confident in what I offer, feel free to make them and then laugh at me. Trust me, I'll be laughing right along with you. Life is nothing if it is not a constant attempt to find the good around us!

Ingredients

Wet

2 eggs, beaten

1 cup milk (whole or 2%)

1 stick butter, melted (8 ounces)

1/2 cup brown sugar, dark

2 tablespoons molasses

1 teaspoon vanilla extract

Dry

2 cups flour, unbleached all-purpose

2 teaspoons ground cinnamon

1 teaspoon ground nutmeg

1 teaspoon baking soda

1/2 teaspoon salt

Directions

Preheat your air fryer to 320°F, setting the timer for enough time to fry all of your donuts.

While your air fryer is preheating, beat the eggs, then mix in the milk, melted butter, brown sugar, molasses, and vanilla extract. In a separate bowl, combine the flour, cinnamon, nutmeg, baking soda, and salt.

Place the batter in a silicon mold or metal donut pan in your air fryer after coating either one lightly with nonstick spray.

Air fry until your donuts are brown, somewhere between 8 and 10 minutes.

Makes 10 to 12 donuts, depending on your mold or pan.

*Note: If you don't have an air fryer, you can still make these in a conventional oven, baking for 7 to 9 minutes at 350°F or until brown.

My Newfangled Bread Pudding

We love bread pudding, ordering it from a local bakery for years until I decided to try to make it myself. I couldn't believe how easy and delicious it was, and I haven't ordered it since! One of the tricks is using stale croissants instead of bread. The butter in them makes them that much more decadent, but if you can't lay your hands on any (I scout my grocery store's discounted bread for them and freeze them whenever they're available), any bread will do. I've used lots of different kinds in the past, but croissants are still my favorite. This is a small recipe, since we tend to eat however much we have, but it can easily be doubled!

Enjoy!

Ingredients

2 whole eggs, room temperature

¾ cup milk plus ¼ cup cream (if you don't have cream, use 1 cup milk, whole, 2% or 1%)

4 ounces melted butter for the mix

¼ cup granulated white sugar

¼ cup brown sugar, light or dark

½ teaspoon vanilla extract

½ teaspoon cinnamon

½ teaspoon nutmeg

4 croissants, stale and cut into chunks

4 ounces melted butter for the top

Directions

In a medium-sized bowl, add the eggs, milk, 4 ounces melted butter, white sugar, brown sugar, vanilla extract, cinnamon, and nutmeg. Mix well.

In a greased 8x8 pan, put the croissant cubes (cubed bread) on the bottom, then pour the liquid mixture over it.

Pour the last 4 ounces of butter over the top and then let it soak for 1 to 3 hours—the longer the better, in my opinion.

Preheat your oven to 350°F and bake for 40 minutes or until it sets up. You can tell by the browning on top and how little the pan jiggles when you shake it, but this is a judgment call, so feel free to experiment here.

Let cool a little and then top with vanilla ice cream. This dessert is also great microwaved later. It's amazing, but for me and my family, the ice cream is what takes it over the top!

Serves four people with reasonable appetites, two of us, or just me if I'm craving bread pudding. Hey, some might call this a single-serving size, so who am I to judge? Been there, done that!

Easy Fried Cherry Pies

SINCE THIS BOOK APPEARS to have a cherry theme (see the first recipe), I decided to offer my easy fried cherry pie recipe. These are some of the easiest things in the world to make, and they are absolutely delicious. Even if you're a seasoned cook, sometimes, a shortcut is still a good thing. Try them, they're worth it!

Ingredients

1 ready-made pie crust

1 can cherry pie filling (15 ounces); I like the one with extra fruit, but that's a personal preference

Enough oil to fry in, peanut or canola

Directions

Let the pie crust thaw a bit, and then roll it onto a lightly floured countertop.

Flour the rim of a bowl or glass approximately 4 inches in diameter and cut circles out of the dough by pressing down and twisting. I usually make four fried pies out of one crust. Place a small amount of pie filling in the center of each circle, then wet the edges of the dough all the way around with water. Fold the dough over in half and pinch the edges together, sealing in the cherry pie filling. The shape will look something like a curved half moon.

Drop the pies into 375°F oil and give them 3 to 4 minutes on each side before turning them with skewers. The crusts will puff out a little along the edges, and they will get golden, with maybe a little brown as well. These usually take about 8 minutes to cook, but the time can vary.

Don't be afraid to leave them in a little longer than you would normally fry something. Pull them from the oil, dust them with powdered sugar, and they're ready to eat.

Makes 4 pies.

If you enjoy Jessica Beck Mysteries and you would like to be notified when the next book is being released, please visit our website at jessicabeckmysteries.net for valuable information about Jessica's books, and sign up for her new-releases-only mail blast.

Your email address will not be shared, sold, bartered, traded, broadcast, or disclosed in any way. There will be no spam from us, just a friendly reminder when the latest book is being released, and of course, you can drop out at any time.

Other Books by Jessica Beck

The Donut Mysteries
Glazed Murder
Fatally Frosted
Sinister Sprinkles
Evil Éclairs
Tragic Toppings
Killer Crullers
Drop Dead Chocolate
Powdered Peril
Illegally Iced
Deadly Donuts
Assault and Batter
Sweet Suspects
Deep Fried Homicide
Custard Crime
Lemon Larceny
Bad Bites
Old Fashioned Crooks
Dangerous Dough
Troubled Treats
Sugar Coated Sins
Criminal Crumbs
Vanilla Vices
Raspberry Revenge
Fugitive Filling
Devil's Food Defense
Pumpkin Pleas
Floured Felonies
Mixed Malice

Tasty Trials
Baked Books
Cranberry Crimes
Boston Cream Bribes
Cherry Filled Charges
Scary Sweets
Cocoa Crush
Pastry Penalties
Apple Stuffed Alibies
Perjury Proof
Caramel Canvas
Dark Drizzles
Counterfeit Confections
Measured Mayhem
Blended Bribes
Sifted Sentences
Dusted Discoveries
Nasty Knead
Rigged Rising
Donut Despair
Whisked Warnings
Baker's Burden
Battered Bluff
The Hole Truth
Donut Disturb
Wicked Wedding Donuts
Donut Hearts Homicide
Sticky Steal
Jelly-Filled Justice
The Classic Diner Mysteries
A Chili Death
A Deadly Beef

A Killer Cake
A Baked Ham
A Bad Egg
A Real Pickle
A Burned Biscuit
The Ghost Cat Cozy Mysteries
Ghost Cat: Midnight Paws
Ghost Cat 2: Bid for Midnight
The Cast Iron Cooking Mysteries
Cast Iron Will
Cast Iron Conviction
Cast Iron Alibi
Cast Iron Motive
Cast Iron Suspicion
Nonfiction
The Donut Mysteries Cookbook